The Manor on the Hill

Iona Stuart

Copyright © 2025 Iona Stuart

All rights reserved

The characters and events portrayed in this book are fictitious. Any similarity to real persons, living or dead, is coincidental and not intended by the author.

No part of this book may be reproduced, or stored in a retrieval system, or transmitted in any form or by any means, electronic, mechanical, photocopying, recording, or otherwise, without express written permission of the publisher.

Contents

Title Page
Copyright

Chapter 1	1
Chapter 2	16
Chapter 3	30
Chapter 4	41
Chapter 5	52
Chapter 6	75
Chapter 7	89
Chapter 8	102
Chapter 9	115
Chapter 10	131
Chapter 11	143
Chapter 12	157
Chapter 13	173
Chapter 14	187

Chapter 14	198
Chapter 16	211
Chapter 17	230
About The Author	247

Chapter 1

A Bride's Arrival

The young girl's emerald eyes flickered back and forth as she drank in the surroundings that were slowly coming into view: the leaves of the parkland trees shimmered lightly in the vast embrace of the midday sun; birds took flight from the overhanging branches, singing sweetly as they passed by on their early bird business; and the large orange glow of Bloodworth manor seemed to come upon her all at once. The trap rolled to a stop. Gravel crunched beneath her feet as she stepped out, the tale of her chauffer's duties being told by the squeaks and scrapes of stone against tiny stone. And there she stood, encircled by luggage, staring up at the stark appearance of the house with a painted face of bewilderment.

The large Edwardian building loomed ahead of her. She traced the tangling lines of red ivy that snaked their way around the drainpipes, clung to the sandstone walls, framed the glass panels around the long windows that ran along the manor. The door was a gaping hole ahead of her, a mouth leading into the void, the land of the unknown, the life that was awaiting her. Then suddenly, the mouth opened, and outstepped three prominent figures.

One of them was clearly the housekeeper. She was a small, portly woman, her stout form adorned with a dark shift, her hands folded politely in front of her. A short wave of greying brown hair floated down around her worn face, and she seemed strangely unmoved by the chill blowing through the bright autumn air. Another was the butler. He was tall, spiny, and grey. What was grey, exactly, Evelyn wasn't entirely sure. It seemed to be his whole being— his skin, his eyes, his demeanour. He looked mute, dumb, like death.

And then there *He* was, standing right in the middle. His imposing frame overshadowed His staff; His black hair was styled perfectly to the side, His dark eyes burrowed into her where she stood. Even from her place beside the car she could sense His stare and only stand there as the heaviness that had suddenly built up in her heart made her nauseous.

She jumped as she felt the touch of a hand upon her back and turned to see her chauffer nod toward the house. She had to take a deep breath in some attempt to calm her nerves. She felt as though she were floating like a feather as she forced one foot in front of the other, her legs made of ice—numb and slow—only aware of her own movement from the crunching of the gravel below, and the impending darkness of her future creeping up closer and closer. And suddenly she was there. He was there. They were there.

"Evelyn Appleby, I presume," the figure spoke.

"Yes." Evelyn watched her breath as it slipped out in light tendrils from her nose, and it wasn't for a moment that she noticed the silence, heard only the cooing of a pigeon in the wind. The man in the middle was looking down at her, as if waiting for something. After a moment of hesitation, she understood.

"Oh," Evelyn breathed, feeling her face flush, and curtsied. She slowly raised her head and looked up at her future husband. Yet, she found she could not look Him in the eye, could not stare into those windows into the abyss, so she averted her gaze to His shirt collar instead.

"Welcome to Bloodworth manor. Maggie here will show you to your room. James, my butler, will arrange for the staff to deliver your belongings." With that, He turned, and retreated back into the grand house, leaving Evelyn standing with her chest pounding.

A whirl of faint steam escaped into the air as she released a breath she hadn't realised she'd been holding, and were it not for the heaviness of her autumn coat holding her down, she was sure she'd drift away.

"Lady Appleby," the housekeeper spoke, "follow me, please."

Evelyn hesitated, looking back once more at the seemingly suddenly familiar face of her chauffer compared to these grandiose strangers. With a shaky breath she nodded lightly to Maggie and followed her into what felt like the lion's den.

The initial darkness of the large doorframe opened up into a large foyer of light. Strips of decorated woodwork lined the walls, cold and rare marble veined with red ran in intricate patterns underfoot, and a showcase adorned with various exotic-looking vases stood between the two winding staircases that framed the grand front hall of the manor house. Keeping a close trot behind the housekeeper, Evelyn followed the small woman up one of the staircases, a plush scarlet runner trailing down the mahogany steps, and down a long corridor that branched off to the right at the top. As she padded hesitantly down the straight expanse that gaped ahead of her, she couldn't help but notice how many doors lined the walls as they passed, wondering just how many intricate mazes lay behind these peculiar wooden barriers; how many lives, how many secrets...

She was so caught up in the daze in her head that she almost walked straight into the back of Maggie as she suddenly came to a stop outside a door at the end of the corridor. The great panel of wood ahead of her was different from the other doors, it was slightly darker in colour, woodwork patterns adorned the frames, and whittled vines of ivy and ringlets of roses were engraved into a mantel, giving the room an air of elegance even before it was glimpsed.

The housekeeper motioned toward the door. "This will be your room, my lady."

Evelyn looked at her for a moment with a blank stare. "Will I not be sharing a bedchamber with the Marquis once we're married?"

"No, miss," Maggie shuffled uncomfortably, as if the very mention of such topics was something she'd rather avoid entirely, "Lord Bloodworth will retain his own chambers and call upon you when... needed."

The young woman felt her eyebrows raise out of her control, wondering (and not for the first time) just what she had gotten herself into, what her parents had gotten her into. With a slight bow of her head, Maggie turned and shuffled away, leaving her alone with her many whirring thoughts as she opened the door ahead of her.

Evelyn, with hesitant steps, crossed the threshold into the gloomy expanse of the gothic-style chamber, her heart echoing the heavy silence that enveloped the room. A shiver coursed through her as the flickering light above her head cast eerie shadows upon the ancient tapestries that adorned the walls, their intricate designs distorted by the dimness. The air seemed laden with secrets, whispers of bygone eras clinging to the musty curtains that veiled the windows. Her gaze swept over the imposing canopy bed, draped in somber hues, its towering frame a stark reminder of the solitude she would endure within these haunted confines.

With a trembling hand, Evelyn brushed aside the heavy curtains, revealing the few strands of afternoon sunlight that filtered through the glass panes, casting a pallid glow upon the worn floorboards. The housekeeper's solemn words echoed in her mind, a chilling reminder of the fate that awaited her in this desolate chamber. It seemed clear to her then that once their marriage was finalised, she would be bound to the whims of the enigmatic Marquis, summoned at His behest to fulfil His desires. As she stood alone in the shadows, a sense of foreboding gripped her soul, and she wondered what dark secrets lay concealed within the walls of her new prison. It was mere minutes later that she was snapped from her thoughts by the sound of heavy hands on her bedroom door.

"Yes?" she called timidly, her voice breaking slightly as she did so.

"Your bags, my lady," came the equally as timid

voice on the other side.

Evelyn hesitated momentarily before gently turning the brass knob of her bedroom door, feeling the weight of apprehension settle upon her delicate shoulders. The dark mahogany door creaked softly as it swung open, revealing the dimly lit expanse of her new abode. Standing in the threshold was a woman who couldn't have been much older than herself, her demeanour poised yet tinged with an air of deference.

"My name is Florence, my lady, one of the housemaids," she said as she extended her arms, bearing the burden of Evelyn's belongings, a tangible manifestation of the transition that awaited her.

As Evelyn's gaze met that of Florence, a silent understanding passed between them, acknowledging the unspoken challenges that lay ahead. With a tentative smile, Evelyn stepped aside, allowing Florence entry into her sanctuary, both women poised at the precipice of an uncertain future.

With measured steps, Florence crossed the threshold into Evelyn's chamber, her movements graceful as she carefully deposited the luggage in a secluded corner, the weight of Evelyn's world neatly contained within the leather confines. As Evelyn watched, a sense of gratitude blossomed within her, tempered by the realisation of the unspoken bond forming between them. Drawing a breath to steady her nerves, Evelyn stepped forward, her voice soft yet resolute as she extended her hand in greeting.

"You don't have to call me 'lady'—my name is Evelyn," she smiled softly, this offer of her Christian name hanging in the air like a fragile promise amidst the uncertainty that enveloped them both. Florence met her gaze with a nod of acknowledgment, unsure just how to feel about that.

With a small smile and bow of the head, much like that previously given by Maggie, the young housemaid turned and shuffled out of the room. As Evelyn delicately undid the clasps on the trunks securing her belongings, her fingers brushed against the polished metal of a music box tucked amidst the folds of her garments. With tender reverence, she lifted the delicate treasure from its resting place, her heart stirring with memories of a simpler time. The tinkling melody that emanated from within the box stirred a bittersweet ache within her soul, reminding her of the fleeting innocence of youth and the impending uncertainties that loomed on the horizon. As the strains of the familiar tune filled the room, Evelyn couldn't help but feel a pang of apprehension gnaw at her resolve, the weight of her impending union with the enigmatic Marquis of Exeter pressing upon her like an unseen shackle.

With trembling hands, Evelyn traced the intricate carvings adorning the music box, each groove a testament to the craftsmanship of a quickly fleeting era. Yet, beneath its ornate façade lay the echoes of her own fears and uncertainties, the song of a silent witness to the tumultuous path that lay ahead floating around the room. As she gazed upon the cherished relic of her past, Evelyn couldn't help but wonder what fate awaited her within the gilded halls of her new home, and whether the melody of her childhood would be drowned out by the discordant strains of a marriage forged in obligation rather than love.

And yet, she could never blame her parents for their choices. As Evelyn sat upon the edge of her bed, cradling the music box in her trembling hands, her thoughts drifted back to her parents, their love a beacon of warmth and security amidst the tumult of her thoughts. They had arranged this marriage with the best of intentions, believing it to be a path to her happiness and security, wanting nothing more than their daughter to have the financial support they could no longer guarantee. Their gentle encouragement had once filled her with hope, but now, as she stared into the uncertain abyss of her future, she couldn't shake the growing realisation that this union held no promise of the happiness she had envisioned. At the tender age of seventeen, the weight of her impending marriage bore down upon her with an oppressive heaviness, suffocating the dreams she had dared to nurture within her heart.

A single tear traced a glistening trail down Evelyn's cheek as she contemplated the stark reality of her situation. The expectations of society, the demands of duty, all seemed to converge upon her with suffocating intensity, leaving her feeling adrift in a sea of uncertainty. The prospect of a life bound to a man she didn't know, whose very name held a sense of foreboding, filled her with a profound sense of dread. In that moment, amidst the hallowed silence of her chamber, Evelyn realised that the sanctuary she had sought in this new home would remain elusive, her spirit tethered to the whims of fate and the dictates of a world that cared naught for the tender desires of a young girl's heart.

As night fell over the imposing manor, Evelyn found herself enveloped in a shroud of eerie solitude, the unfamiliar creaks and whispers of the old house echoing like ghostly murmurs throughout the corridors. Beneath the weight of the heavy brocade covers, sleep eluded her, her mind haunted by visions of a future cloaked in uncertainty. The flickering candlelight from her bedside table cast dancing shadows upon the walls, each one a reminder of the looming spectre of her impending marriage.

With the first light of dawn, Evelyn rose from

her restless slumber, steeling herself for the day ahead. As if in answer to her silent prayers, a knock resounded upon her chamber door, heralding the arrival of Maggie, whose surprisingly almost comforting presence offered a glimmer of solace amidst the oppressive atmosphere of the manor. With a gentle smile, Maggie nodded politely, her warm demeanour a welcome respite from the chill that lingered within the old walls.

"Good morning, my lady," the housekeeper began, "I've been tasked with showing you around your new home."

Evelyn smiled and nodded politely in response, taking a deep breath as she followed the older woman out of the room.

Together, they embarked upon a tour of the main parts of the manor, Maggie's steady voice guiding Evelyn through the labyrinthine corridors and opulent chambers with an air of quiet authority. Yet, beneath the veneer of grandeur, Evelyn couldn't shake the sense of unease that gnawed at her spirit, the whispered secrets of the manor stirring a disquiet within her soul.

As Maggie led Evelyn through the maze of corridors, they passed by several spare bedrooms, each adorned with antique furnishings and faded tapestries that spoke of a splendour that had once been so much more than the one it held to that day (a surprising thought).

"These rooms have seen many guests over the years," Maggie remarked, her voice tinged with a hint of nostalgia. "But none so important as you, my Lady."

Evelyn offered a tentative smile in response, her thoughts drifting to the daunting prospect of becoming the mistress of this sprawling estate.

Their journey continued down a grand staircase adorned with an ornate mahogany banister, the same one she'd been led up the day before with its scarlet runner, leading them to the imposing oak door that marked the entrance to Lord Bloodworth's private quarters. Maggie paused, her gaze lingering upon the threshold with a mixture of reverence and apprehension.

"This is the wing belonging to the Marquis," she explained, her tone hushed as if speaking in reverence of a sacred relic. "But we mustn't disturb him without cause."

Evelyn nodded in understanding, a shiver running down her spine as she contemplated the enigmatic figure who awaited her within those forbidding walls.

Their tour continued through the opulent dining room, where a grand table stretched out beneath a crystal chandelier that cast a warm glow upon the polished silverware and fine china adorning its surface.

"Here is where you will preside over many a grand dinner for your guests," Maggie remarked, her eyes alight with anticipation. From there, they made their way to the bustling heart of the manor —the kitchen—where the staff worked tirelessly to prepare meals fit for royalty. The scent of freshly baked bread mingled with the aroma of savoury stews, enveloping Evelyn in a comforting embrace that momentarily eased her troubled mind.

As they ventured into the library, Evelyn's heart quickened with excitement at the sight of row upon row of leather-bound tomes lining the shelves.

"This is where you will find all the books of the house, the shelves cleaned and dusted daily, as most of our rooms are," Maggie said, her voice soft with reverence for the wisdom contained within those hallowed walls. Finally, they arrived at the parlour, a sanctuary of plush armchairs and intricately embroidered cushions where guests were entertained amidst the flickering flames of a roaring fireplace.

"Here is where memories are made," Maggie declared, her eyes alight with a warmth that belied the solemnity of their surroundings. As Evelyn took in the splendour of her new home, a sense of determination welled within her, tempered by the knowledge that amidst the old grandeur and the uncertainty, she would find the path to carve out her own destiny.

As they made their way back upstairs towards Evelyn's bedroom, she noticed out of the corner of her eye that the door to the Marquis' wing they'd past earlier now lay open, and at the very end of the hallway behind, she spied an ornate door. Turning her head for a better view, she could just make out that the door was adorned with a large lock just below the brass handle.

"Maggie," she asked, coming to a stop, "what's in there?"

Maggie froze, her face suddenly contorted into a look of hesitance and trepidation as she hurried to close the door that led to the forbidden corridor. "I'm sorry, my lady, but we do not enter these rooms."

Evelyn parted her lips slightly as though to enquire further, but the look on the housekeeper's face told her that this was not something to be investigated more.

"Come, my lady, let's get you ready for the day."

Evelyn couldn't shake the sense of curiosity that gnawed at her as she thought upon the mysterious door she'd glimpsed, its imposing lock a silent sentinel guarding the secrets within. Yet, the haunted expression that flickered across Maggie's features served as a stark reminder that some mysteries were best left undisturbed. With a reluctant nod, Evelyn allowed herself to be led away, the unanswered questions lingering like shadows in the recesses of her mind. As they continued back towards Evelyn's chamber, she couldn't shake the feeling that behind that locked door lay secrets that could unravel the delicate tapestry of her newfound existence.

But for now, she pushed aside her unease, resolving to focus on the task at hand—to navigate the labyrinthine corridors of her new home with courage and grace, even as the spectre of uncertainty loomed large on the horizon.

Chapter 2

A Wedding of Shadows

The next week came and went in what felt like the blink of an eye and an eternity all at once. Evelyn found herself swept up in a whirlwind of preparations for her impending wedding to the elusive Marquis of Exeter. As she sat before the ornate vanity mirror in her chamber, her reflection gazing back at her with a mixture of trepidation and anticipation, Maggie bustled about, fastening the final buttons of Evelyn's long white gown with practiced precision.

"You look positively radiant, my lady," Maggie remarked, her voice tinged with a hint of admiration. "I dare say the Marquis won't know what to think when he sees you."

Evelyn offered a nervous smile in response, her fingers trembling as she clasped the delicate bouquet of blood-red roses that lay nestled in her lap, not sure she believed that at all. Equally unsure if that was a compliment at all. And knowing perfectly well that she also had no idea what to think.

"I can only hope He finds me pleasing enough," she murmured, the weight of uncertainty pressing upon her young mind like a leaden cloak. Maggie's gentle laughter filled the chamber, a reassuring melody amidst the sea of doubts that threatened to engulf Evelyn's fragile resolve.

"Trust me, my lady, you will be the belle of the ball," she assured, her unwavering confidence a beacon of reassurance in the stormy sea of Evelyn's thoughts. As they made their way towards the grand hall where the ceremony awaited, Evelyn couldn't help but cling to Maggie's words like a lifeline, praying that amidst the pomp and pageantry of the day, she would find the strength to face the uncertain future that lay ahead.

As Evelyn stepped into the grand hall, her heart fluttered nervously within her chest at the sight that greeted her. The room was adorned with opulent tapestries and the flickering candlelight of a million little tealights, casting a warm glow upon the assembled guests who whispered and murmured amongst themselves in hushed tones. At the head of the hall stood the imposing figure of the Marquis. As Evelyn approached, a wave of apprehension washed over her, her gaze sweeping over the sea of unfamiliar faces that filled the hall.

At Lord Bloodworth's side stood the venerable priest, his solemn visage a testament to the sanctity of the occasion. As the strains of a haunting melody filled the air, Evelyn felt a gentle pressure on her arm, and she turned to find herself face to face with her betrothed. Marquis Julien Bloodworth of Exeter—as this was all she could possibly see herself regarding Him as—looked at her with an inscrutable expression, His piercing gaze seeming to bore into her very soul.

"You look exquisite, my dear," He murmured, His voice low and velvety, sending an oddly uncomfortable shiver down Evelyn's spine.

"Thank you, my Lord," Evelyn replied, her voice barely above a whisper as she fought to keep her composure amidst the overwhelming splendour of the moment. With a nod of acknowledgment, the Marquis turned towards the priest, signalling the beginning of the ceremony. As the priest began to recite the solemn vows that would bind them together for eternity, Evelyn felt as though time stood still, the weight of their words hanging heavy in the air like a sacred promise she wasn't sure she wanted to make.

Around them, the guests watched with rapt attention, their eyes alight with curiosity and intrigue as they bore witness to the union of houses. Among them, Evelyn recognised the faces of distant relatives and esteemed acquaintances of the Marquis (and yet, none of her own), their expressions a mixture of polite interest and veiled scrutiny. As the ceremony drew to a close and the final vows were exchanged, Evelyn felt a sense of surreal detachment wash over her, as though she were merely a spectator in her own life, caught up in the currents of fate beyond her control.

"I, Evelyn Appleby, take you, Lord Julien Bloodworth, the Marquis of Exeter, to be my lawfully wedded husband, to have and to hold from this day forward, for better, for worse, for richer, for poorer, in sickness and in health, to love and to cherish, till death us do part, according to God's holy law, and this is my solemn vow." She felt the words leave her mouth in a stream of noise that felt like it lived of its own accord, completely detached from her own person.

As the newlyweds exchanged a chaste kiss beneath the gaze of their assembled guests, Evelyn couldn't help but wonder what lay in store for her in the days and years to come. Amidst the grandeur and the glamour of her new life as the Marchioness of Exeter, she couldn't shake the nagging feeling that beneath the façade of their fairytale romance lurked shadows of doubt and uncertainty. Yet, as she gazed into the enigmatic depths of her husband's dark eyes, she found a glimmer of hope amidst the uncertainty—a silent promise of love yet to be discovered amidst the tangled web of their intertwined destinies.

And, as the moment occurred, Evelyn Appleby died forever, replaced for eternity by Lady Evelyn Bloodworth of Bloodworth Manor, Marchioness of Exeter.

With the end of the ceremony, the guests drifted into the sumptuous reception hall of the manor, where the opulence of the occasion rivalled the grandeur of the ceremony itself. Evelyn found herself adrift amidst a sea of unfamiliar faces, the strains of polite conversation and laughter echoing like distant whispers in her ears. She stood at the edge of the great room, her fingers delicately toying with the lace of her gown, feeling the weight of her new title settling uneasily upon her shoulders.

"Lord Julien, this gathering is truly a splendid affair," remarked one Sir, a distinguished guest whose presence commanded attention amidst the assembled company. His voice carried across the room, drawing the gaze of those nearby, including Evelyn and the Marquis Himself. "A union of noble houses, indeed."

Evelyn felt her delicate heart race at the expectation that her own house was ever that noble. If anything, the very need for this arranged marriage must surely prove the opposite. The Marquis nodded graciously in acknowledgment, His demeanour exuding an air of effortless charm as He exchanged pleasantries with said Sir and the other illustrious guests who vied for His attention. Evelyn observed from a distance, her heart heavy with a sense of apprehension as she struggled to find her footing amidst the elegance and formality of the occasion. Be it her own wedding or not. It certainly seemed as if not.

"Lady Evelyn, you look positively radiant," remarked another Lady she did not know, a striking figure whose grace and poise marked her as a seasoned member of high society. She approached Evelyn with a warm smile, her eyes sparkling with recognition as she took in Evelyn's uncertain demeanour. "There's no need to worry, my dear. You are among friends here."

Evelyn offered a tentative smile in response, her gratitude mingled with a profound sense of vulnerability as she found herself drawn into this Lady's presence, insinuating an air of reassurance, but Evelyn couldn't be sure. She, herself, was the true stranger here, after all.

"Thank you," she murmured, her voice betraying a hint of uncertainty as she navigated the unfamiliar intricacies of social etiquette. Yet, amidst the sea of grandiose strangers and whispered conversations, Evelyn couldn't shake the feeling of isolation that pervaded the room, a silent reminder of the solitary journey that lay ahead as the Marchioness of Exeter.

As Evelyn navigated the maze of unfamiliar faces and hushed conversations, her gaze fell upon a younger-looking gentleman who stood apart from the throng, his countenance marked by an air of quiet contemplation. Clad in a tailored suit of somber hues, he exuded an aura of understated elegance that captivated her attention. Sensing her scrutiny, the gentleman turned, revealing a pair of keen blue eyes that sparkled with intelligence beneath a thick mane of blond hair. With a courteous nod, he acknowledged her presence before extending a hand in greeting.

"Lady Evelyn," he smiled, his voice a melodic cadence that bespoke refinement and warmth in equal measure. "Archibald Bates—though, everyone calls me Archie—cousin to your esteemed new husband. It is a pleasure to make your acquaintance."

His words carried a sincerity that resonated with Evelyn, dispelling the lingering apprehension that had clouded her thoughts. Grateful for what seemed like a genuine kindness amidst the sea of strangers, she returned his gesture with a graceful nod, her spirits lifted by the prospect of finding solace in the company of a kindred spirit amidst the opulent splendour of high society.

With a gentle smile gracing her lips, Evelyn shook his hand in a timid gesture of camaraderie, meeting Archie's with a delicate touch that stirred the air with unspoken allure.

"It is indeed a pleasure to make your acquaintance, Mr. Bates," she murmured softly, her voice carrying a hint of nervousness veiled by the grace of her demeanour. In that fleeting moment of connection, Evelyn sensed an indefinable spark between them; a subtle recognition that almost made her feel at ease.

Archie's gaze, warm and penetrating, held hers in a silent exchange fraught with unspoken meaning. In his presence, Evelyn found herself enveloped in a newfound sense of belonging, as if she had stumbled upon a kindred spirit amidst the whirlwind of wedding festivities that barely seemed to include her. For she was only the bride, after all.

Amidst the opulent splendour of the wedding celebrations as they continued, Evelyn stole furtive glances at this intriguing Mr. Bates, her heart quickening with a mingling of anticipation and trepidation. And though their encounter was brief, it left an indelible imprint upon her soul, igniting a flame of longing that danced upon the edges of propriety, whispering of forbidden desires.

And then, out of nowhere, he approached.

He took a step toward her, wrapping his large arms around her waist, and looked down at the Lady Bloodworth. His deep eyes gazed into hers as his brow furrowed. His lips opened, and her heart jumped in her chest. He was magnificent.

"Lady Evelyn," his voice rippled into her ears, "may I have this dance?"

In that moment, Evelyn could do nothing but stare, and nod, words having abandoned her completely.

As the opulence of the wedding festivities faded into the quiet of the night, Lord Julien escorted Evelyn through the ornate corridors of the manor, His hand resting possessively on her arm as they ascended the staircase towards His private chambers. Evelyn's heart fluttered nervously within her chest, the undeniable feeling of anxiety coursing through her veins as they approached the threshold of their new life together.

Once inside the dimly lit chamber that was otherwise off limits, Lord Julien turned to face Evelyn, His eyes dark with desire as He closed the distance between them with purposeful strides. Evelyn's breath caught in her throat as she felt His hands graze her skin, His touch sending a shiver of apprehension down her spine. She had dreamed of this moment, of sharing herself with her husband in a union of love and tenderness. But as Lord Julien's lips found hers with a hunger that bordered on aggression, she couldn't shake the feeling that something was amiss, as she'd felt ever since their first meeting.

With a swift movement, Lord Julien began to disrobe her, His hands rough and impatient as He stripped away the layers of silk and lace that adorned Evelyn's trembling form. The air was thick with a tension that hung between them, the weight of expectation giving way to a palpable sense of unease as she found herself succumbing to His advances with a mixture of fear and resignation.

As His hands roamed over Evelyn's youthful body, His touch was both possessive and probing, tracing the contours of her form with in such a way that sent a shiver down her spine. His gaze, sharp and invasive, lingered upon her with an intensity that made her feel exposed, laid bare beneath His unwavering scrutiny. With each caress, Evelyn felt a sense of vulnerability wash over her, her breath catching in her throat as she struggled to maintain her composure under His relentless gaze.

As He continued to undress her, Lord Julien's disposition remained impassive, His expression betraying none of the turmoil that raged within Evelyn's heart. His hands moved with a precision that bordered on ruthlessness, stripping away the last vestiges of her modesty until she stood before Him, naked and vulnerable, a mere pawn in His game of desire. And though her body trembled with a mixture of anticipation and apprehension, Evelyn dared not protest, resigned to her fate as she surrendered herself to His will.

With a predatory gleam in His eyes, Lord Julien drew closer, His breath hot against her skin as He claimed her with a possessiveness that left no room for doubt. In that moment of carnal abandon, Evelyn felt herself consumed by a tumultuous whirlwind of sensation, her senses overwhelmed by the raw intensity of their union. And as their bodies entwined in a desperate embrace, she could not help but wonder if she would ever find solace amidst the tangled web of desire and deceit that bound her to this man. And, in that moment, her mind wandered, disappeared to a place inside herself that blocked out the world around her, taking her somewhere new inside her brain that brought her comfort.

That night He claimed her with a ferocity that left her breathless and bewildered, Evelyn's mind reeling with a whirlwind of conflicting emotions. She had imagined their first night together as a tender exchange of love and intimacy, a culmination of the vows they had spoken earlier that day. But instead, she found herself consumed by a feeling of emptiness and disillusionment, her body yielding to His desires even as her heart cried out for something more.

In the aftermath of their intensity, as Evelyn lay spent and vulnerable in the silence of the Lord's chambers, He broke the stillness with a voice that cut through the darkness like a blade.

"You should return to your own bedroom," He said, his tone devoid of warmth or tenderness. And as Evelyn gathered her scattered garments and made her way back through the labyrinthine corridors of the manor, she couldn't shake the feeling that she had lost something precious in the dark recesses of the night—a piece of herself that could never be reclaimed. And in that moment, amidst the silence that stretched between them like an unbridgeable chasm, she realised that the fairytale romance she had once dreamed of was nothing more than a distant illusion, shattered by the harsh reality of her new life as the Marchioness of Exeter.

The night passed faster than she first imagined as she cried into the warmth of her pillow, the only warmth she had felt so far within the encompassing walls of the dark manor. Except, maybe, in her fleeting conversation with the intriguing Lord Archibald Bates, a figure unlike all the rest that she was rather sure she'd never come across again. As the sun streamed in from the cracks in the heavy curtains, illuminating the many specs of dust as they danced their own waltz around her chamber, Evelyn sighed heavily and rose from her bed, entirely unsure of what she was supposed to do now. Just as these thoughts crossed her mind, she was interrupted by a knock at the door, after which entered Maggie, without waiting for a response from within.

"Good morning, Lady Bloodworth," Maggie greeted warmly, despite the fact that her new title sent shivers down her spine. "It's time to start the day."

Evelyn offered a weak smile in return, grateful for Maggie's steady presence.

"Shall I prepare the shower for you, my Lady?" Maggie enquired; her tone gentle but firm, indicating that this was not so much a question than a request.

Evelyn hesitated briefly before nodding her assent, grateful for the prospect of the warm water washing away the traces of her troubled thoughts, as well as the inexplicable shame she'd felt run through her entire body since the previous night. As Maggie left the room to attend to her duties, Evelyn made her way to the grand bathroom, its marble floors gleaming in the morning light.

With a sense of anticipation, Evelyn stepped into the shower, feeling the warm water cascade over her weary body. As the steam enveloped her, she closed her eyes, allowing herself a moment of respite from the worries that plagued her mind.

The miniature crystalline droplets fell upon her from their stream above, raining down into the deepest crevices of her darkened mind; their iridescence striking through her ruined temple, until reaching the surface of her shining soul. Hundreds of beaded diamonds rolled down the slope of her skin, still taught and fresh with the impatience of youth, sliding slowly over her budding breasts, trickling between her thighs. The evanescent wall of mist reflected the stark nature of her form, revealed at once for inspection. She ran her delicate fingers over the bump of her pink nipple, like an artist examining his portrait for the first time. Her head began to fill with the incessant pattering of a hundred thousand tears dropping all at once. Taking the tip of her index finger, she gently removed a layer of moisture from the shrouded wall of sparkling lights, and with a squeak inscribed simply one word upon its surface, asking only: '*How?*'

How was it so different here by the way He touched her? The way He had done so only the night before. The way He had examined her with the intense scrutiny of an anatomist dissecting his one true love. And for the first time, she had looked at Him with a sense of dispassionate clarity; she had seen the glimpse of the man behind the curtain, and of the beast within the man. He had run his rough thumbs over the soft tissue of her girl's breasts, and they had hardened to His touch.

She inhaled deeply, the lines of her ribcage straining against the barrier of her wet, translucent skin, the cavern of her chest drawing deeper into itself, until she felt she might burst.

Chapter 3

The Brutal Truth

Another night passed, and the morning sky broke into the world once more. The harsh light of day poured onto Evelyn's face from the crack in the heavy curtains that hung from the brass rungs, illuminating her pallid features as it danced over her stirring body. Her eyelids opened to the new world around her, as her ears opened to the deathly silence that seemed to have captivated her surroundings. This was how she'd awoken every morning since… since He'd taken it. Awaking to the deep nothingness the world held, where noise was non-existent, and light was somehow both dull and blinding against the empty reality in which she was forced to walk around.

She'd spent many of those first days just lying there, oblivious to everything around her, not hearing the sounds of the grand house that surrounded her, not feeling the embrace of the duck down duvet above her. She didn't eat; the silver trays of food piled up throughout the day and were removed almost untouched each night. She barely slept, just lay, and stared. And yet, somehow, on this day, she managed to get up. She couldn't hide from Him forever.

Her head began to spin as soon as she reached her new position. It would seem that simply being upright was now a chore, and she had no-one but herself to blame for that. She swayed slightly where she sat, watching as the world slowly drifted back into focus, and wriggled her toes lightly against the soft rug beneath her delicate feet.

It was strange to see and feel the hard embrace of the world in which she now found herself living, and not feel it crumble from under her, but instead to be faced with the harsh reality that this was how things were now, and nothing she said or did or even felt would ever change that.

She wandered downstairs for the first time in days in what felt like a dream, as if she were simply floating around the manor she was now expected to call home; a living ghost haunting her own life. The red runner passed beneath her feet in a blur, like wafting through a river of blood. She was now Lady Bloodworth, after all.

The very air around her felt different as she descended the staircase, a mingling of scents wafting from the kitchens below as she went in search of Maggie, the one person she knew was still there, somewhere. Upon entering the kitchen, Evelyn was greeted by the warmth of the hearth and the bustling activity of the household staff. The housekeeper looked up from her tasks with a gentle smile, her eyes betraying a hint of concern.

"Good morning, Lady Evelyn," Maggie greeted her, her voice a welcome reassurance amidst the unfamiliarity of the surroundings.

Evelyn returned the greeting with a hesitant nod, her gaze fixed upon Maggie's familiar countenance. It had been too long since she had ventured beyond the confines of her chamber; too long since she had faced the reality of her new life. A week had never felt just so long as it has these past seven days, which had felt more like seven years.

As she busied herself with a task at one of the large ovens that adorned the kitchen, Maggie's gaze softened with empathy.

"I must confess, Lady Evelyn," she began, her tone gentle yet somber, as if able to read what was going through her mistresses's mind, "you are not likely to see Lord Julien very often."

Evelyn's heart sank at the admission, despite having felt since her arrival that this would be the case, a pang of loneliness gripping her soul; not so much for the absence of her husband, but more for what seemed like the absence of any human soul. She had known, of course, that her marriage to Lord Julien was one simply made of decency and contract, but the reality of her situation was still new to her. There had always been the hope that it could become something more, but, since her wedding night, she knew this could never be the truth. Not now that she'd had a taste of his beastliness.

"Lord Julien is a man of many responsibilities," Maggie continued, her voice tinged with sympathy." His duties often keep him occupied, leaving little time for personal matters."

With a heavy sigh, Evelyn nodded in understanding, though the ache of disappointment lingered in her heart. She had hoped, perhaps naïvely, that marriage would bring her the companionship and solace she so desperately craved. Yet, as she stood amidst the warmth and bustle of the kitchen, she knew that her journey towards fulfillment would be one she must undertake alone.

As Evelyn lingered in the kitchen, her thoughts weighed heavy with the revelation from Maggie regarding Lord Julien's frequent absences. It was then that a movement caught her eye—a figure darting through the doorway, her movements swift and furtive. It was Florence, a young housemaid, not much older than herself, whom Evelyn had seen bustle around her a few times since her arrival at the manor.

Their eyes met briefly, a silent exchange passing between them before Florence averted her gaze, her cheeks flushed with embarrassment. Sensing an opportunity to glean more insight into her enigmatic husband's whereabouts, Evelyn approached the young maid with cautious curiosity.

"Florence," Evelyn called softly, her voice barely above a whisper. "Might I have a moment of your time?"

Startled, Florence turned to face Evelyn, her expression a mixture of surprise and trepidation. Yet, as Evelyn regarded her with gentle understanding, the young maid relented, her curiosity piqued by the earnestness in Evelyn's eyes.

Drawing closer, Evelyn spoke in hushed tones, her words a delicate dance of inquiry and intrigue. "I couldn't help but notice your hesitance, Florence," she began, her voice barely audible above the hum of activity in the kitchen. "Do you know anything about Lord Julien's activities?"

At first, Florence hesitated, her gaze darting nervously about the room as if searching for an escape. Yet, with a deep breath, she summoned the courage to speak, her words tumbling forth in a rush of revelation.

"Lord Julien," Florence began, her voice barely above a whisper, "he frequents the Gentlemen's Clubs in the city, and sometimes he brings back other lords and… young girls."

Evelyn's heart quickened at the revelation, a mix of shock and disbelief coursing through her veins. She had known Lord Julien to be a man of influence and prestige, but the notion of him engaging in such clandestine activities filled her with a sense of unease.

"And the locked wing upstairs," Florence continued, her voice trembling with apprehension. "He takes them there, behind closed doors, and they do not emerge until morning… if they emerge at all. And I'm not the only one who's noticed."

Evelyn's mind raced with possibilities; her thoughts consumed by the secrets that lay hidden within the walls of the manor. She'd so wondered about the door to the wing Maggie would not speak of… and what she'd glimpsed of the door at the end of the forbidden corridor. With each passing moment, the truth of her husband's character became increasingly elusive, leaving her to wonder what other mysteries lay concealed beneath the façade of propriety and privilege.

"Thank you, Florence," she whispered in reply. "You'd better get back to your duties before Maggie notices."

Florence nodded in understanding and quickly headed back toward the centre of the bustling kitchen duties that awaited her. As Evelyn absorbed these revelations, her mind churned with a tumult of emotions. Uncertainty gnawed at her, mingling with a burgeoning sense of apprehension.

With a heavy heart, Evelyn bid farewell to Florence, her thoughts consumed by the weight of the knowledge she had gained. As she made her way through the corridors of the manor, her steps echoed with the rhythm of her racing thoughts. She needed answers, clarity amidst the confusion that clouded her perception of her husband.

The library beckoned to her like a sanctuary amidst the storm, its shelves laden with volumes of knowledge and wisdom. With each step, Evelyn felt a sense of solace wash over her, the familiar scent of leather-bound books offering a welcome respite from the chaos of her thoughts.

As she entered, Evelyn's gaze swept across the rows of shelves, searching for any escape amidst the pages that lay within. She selected a tome at random, its spine worn with age and wisdom, and sank into the plush embrace of an armchair.

Lost in the labyrinth of her thoughts, rather than the labyrinth of the manor, Evelyn delved into the pages before her, seeking solace in the wisdom of the written word. With each passing moment, she couldn't help but find her mind drifting back to the enigmatic figure of Lord Julien, His presence looming large in her thoughts like a shadow cast across her heart.

In the quiet solitude of the library, Evelyn inhaled the scent of the volume in her hands with the determined vigour of an opium addict. Looking down at the title properly for the first time, she traced her fingers over the grooves in the leather that spelt out, 'A Midsummer Night's Dream', and smiled. As she immersed herself in the pages of Shakespeare, she found herself transported to a world of enchantment and whimsy. The words danced before her eyes, weaving a tapestry of magic and romance that captured her imagination in its spell.

Lost amidst the antics of Oberon, Titania, and the mischievous Puck, Evelyn felt a sense of liberation wash over her. For in the realm of the written word, she found solace from the complexities of her own reality, a fleeting escape from the burdens that weighed heavily upon her heart.

As she followed the twists and turns of the plot, Evelyn discovered parallels between the characters' trials and tribulations and her own struggles. Like Hermia, she found herself caught in the throes of love and duty, torn between the expectations of society and the desires of her heart.

Amidst the chaos of the fairytale kingdom and the mortal realm, Evelyn found moments of levity and joy that lifted her spirits. The playful banter of the lovers and the whimsical antics of Bottom and his fellow actors brought a smile to her lips, reminding her of the simple pleasures that could be found amidst life's trials.

In the world of Shakespeare's creation, Evelyn found refuge from the uncertainties that plagued her mind. For a brief moment, she was able to set aside the burdens of her own reality and lose herself in the timeless beauty of the written word. And as she turned the pages of the play, she felt a glimmer of hope ignite within her soul, a reminder that even in the darkest of times, there is always light to be found in the power of literature and imagination.

As the hours passed in the comforting embrace of the library, Evelyn found herself drawn deeper into the world of Shakespeare's enchanting tale. The sun cast its warm glow through the tall windows, painting the room in hues of gold and amber as she turned page after page, losing herself in the timeless story unfolding before her.

Lost in the beautiful web of words, Evelyn scarcely noticed as the shadows lengthened and the daylight began to fade. It was only when the soft glow of lamplight flickered to life within the library that she reluctantly tore herself away from the pages, realising that the day had waned into evening.

With a heavy heart, Evelyn rose from her seat, her thoughts lingering on the mysteries that still awaited her beyond the confines of the library walls. Yet, as she made her way down the long red runner toward her room, a flicker of movement caught her eye—a figure lurking in the shadows, concealed from view.

Drawing closer, Evelyn's heart quickened with a sense of foreboding as she recognised the familiar form of her husband standing near the entrance to His secret wing. Beside Him stood a young girl, her features obscured by the dim light, yet her presence sending a shiver down Evelyn's spine.

In the stillness of the moment, Evelyn remained rooted to the spot, her gaze fixed upon the clandestine scene unfolding before her. There was an air of urgency in Lord Julien's demeanour as he pulled the young girl into the hidden chamber, His movements swift and decisive, betraying a sense of secrecy that sent alarm bells ringing in Evelyn's mind.

For a moment, time seemed to stand still as Evelyn grappled with the implications of what she had witnessed. In the darkness of the corridor, the truth hung heavy in the air, casting a pall of uncertainty over her once hopeful heart.

With a heavy sigh, Evelyn tore her gaze away from the scene before her, a sense of betrayal gnawing at her soul. As she made her way back towards her room, the weight of the knowledge she had gained pressed heavily upon her, casting a shadow over the fragile façade of her newfound sanctuary. And as she retreated into the solitude of her own chamber, Evelyn knew that the secrets of the manor would continue to haunt her dreams, long into the night.

Chapter 4

The Forbidden Wing

The first few months following the wedding, her realisations crept by in anything other than wedded bliss. Evelyn, once accustomed to the warm chaos of her modest family home with her parents and her younger sister, found herself adrift in the cavernous silence of Bloodworth Manor. The air felt colder here, weighted with a past she could not see but sensed in every creak of the floorboards and whisper of the wind against frosted windowpanes. The staff scurried about like shadows, their gazes averted when she passed, and conversations died on their lips as though even her presence was unwelcome or dangerous.

Julien was not a cruel husband in any overt manner—no bruising words or raised hands marred her days with Him. But there was a hardness to Him, an unrelenting coldness that coated every word and gesture like frost on iron. He treated her less as a partner and more as another piece of His estate: valuable when polished, yet wholly functional, expected to serve its purpose without complaint or need.

In those months, Evelyn had learnt to keep quiet, to avert her eyes and simply get on with it, to hold her tongue and nod in response to His demands, unquestioning. But her mind never stopped wondering. She'd even given up writing home, knowing perfectly well that it would make no difference. What could they do now that they couldn't have done before her nuptials? There was a reason she had been sent there, after all, and she must do her part.

Evelyn's fingers trembled as they traced the ornate carvings on the threshold of what she'd quickly come to realise was a part of the house from which she was forbidden from entering. The air hung heavy with silence, broken only by the rapid drumming of her heart. She cast a furtive glance over her shoulder, her deep green eyes scanning the empty corridor behind her.

"I shouldn't be here," she whispered, her voice barely audible. Yet, the allure of the unknown proved too strong to resist.

Taking a deep breath, Evelyn pushed open the heavy wooden door, and stepped into the dimly lit passageway. The floorboards creaked beneath her feet, and she winced at the sound. Her hand instinctively flew to her throat, fingering a delicate pearl necklace that had been a wedding gift from

Julien, like a white collar she couldn't take off.

"What secrets are you hiding, my dear husband?" she mused, her tone a mixture of curiosity and trepidation.

As she ventured deeper into the wing, Evelyn's footsteps echoed softly against the stone floor. The portraits lining the walls seemed to watch her every move, their eyes following her progress. She shivered, pulling her shawl tighter around her shoulders.

"You are Lady Bloodworth now," she reminded herself, squaring her shoulders. "You have every right to be here. No matter what they might say."

But even as she spoke the words, doubt gnawed at her. The faces in the portraits wore expressions of disapproval, as if chastising her for her boldness. Evelyn's gaze lingered on a particularly stern-looking woman, her grey eyes piercing even through the veil of dust.

I wonder, Evelyn heard the voice say inside, studying the portrait, *did you also marry into this family? Did you, too, feel like an outsider in your own home?*

She shook her head, pushing away the melancholy thoughts. Her curiosity had brought her this far; she wouldn't turn back now. With each step, Evelyn felt a strange mix of exhilaration and dread. What lay at the end of this corridor? Where did that door truly lead? What secrets would she uncover?

As Evelyn reached the final wooded precipice, her

breath caught in her throat. Before her stood an imposing door, its dark wood scarred with age and adorned with intricate iron scrollwork. The sight of it made her heart race, a mixture of anticipation and fear coursing through her veins.

With trembling fingers, she reached out to touch the cold iron handle. A shiver ran down her spine at the contact, as if the door itself was warning her away. Evelyn hesitated, her hand still on the handle.

"What are you doing?" she questioned herself, her blazing green eyes wide with uncertainty. "If the Marquis were to find out..."

But even as the thought crossed her mind, her curiosity surged forward, drowning out her fears. She had come too far to turn back now. Her fingers tightened on the handle, but it refused to budge.

"Locked," she murmured, a mix of disappointment and relief in her voice. As if she could ever have thought anything different from the obvious lock on the outside. Any yet... a part of her thought it was only for show, like a lot of the old manor had proved to be.

Evelyn's gaze dropped to the large keyhole below the obvious lock, dark and inviting. She bit her lip, warring with herself. Should she dare to look? What secrets lay beyond this threshold? Surely it meant nothing? Especially since how thick the chain in front of her appeared to be. Then again...

Slowly, deliberately, she lowered herself to peer through the keyhole, her heart pounding so loudly she was sure it would betray her presence to anyone nearby.

And for a moment, for a split moment, she saw something. What she saw, she couldn't quite say. A woman? Two women? Red? Orange? Brown? She wasn't sure. It was dark. But bricks. She saw bricks. A brick room, of that, she was certain.

Just as Evelyn's eye aligned with the keyhole, a sudden flurry of hurried footsteps echoed through the corridor from behind her. Of that, she was certain. She froze, her breath catching in her throat.

"Lady Bloodworth!" Maggie's voice rang out, uncharacteristically shrill. "Step away from that door, I beg you!"

Evelyn whirled around, her dark hair fanning out as she faced the approaching housekeeper. Maggie's usually calm demeanour had vanished, replaced by an expression of naked anxiety that sent a chill through Evelyn's core.

"Maggie?" Evelyn managed, her voice barely above a whisper. "Whatever is the matter?"

The portly woman hurried towards her, hands outstretched as if to physically pull Evelyn away from the door.

"Please, my lady," Maggie pleaded, her voice trembling. "You mustn't be here. It's not safe."

Evelyn took an involuntary step back, her curiosity now mingling with a growing sense of unease. "Not safe? Maggie, what do you mean?"

Maggie's eyes darted nervously between Evelyn

and the locked door. "I... I can't explain, my lady. But please, we must leave this place at once."

As Evelyn studied the housekeeper's face, she noticed beads of sweat forming on Maggie's brow. This was so unlike the composed woman she had come to know in the past few months. What could possibly have her so rattled?

"Maggie," Evelyn said, straightening her posture and trying to infuse her voice with the quiet authority she'd started trying to cultivate as Lady Bloodworth. "Tell me what's behind this door."

Maggie's eyes flickered to the locked door once more, and in that brief glance, Evelyn caught a glimpse of raw fear that made her breath catch. The housekeeper's usual warm brown eyes were wide and glassy, filled with an emotion that went beyond mere anxiety.

"*My lady,*" Maggie whispered, her voice quavering, "*some secrets are best left undisturbed. For your own safety, I implore you to forget about this wing.*"

Evelyn felt a chill run down her spine. The room beyond that door suddenly seemed to pulse with a sinister energy she hadn't noticed before. What horrors could it possibly contain to elicit such a reaction from the normally unflappable housekeeper?

"But Maggie, I—" Evelyn began, her resolve weakening in the face of the housekeeper's palpable distress.

"Please, Lady Bloodworth," Maggie interrupted,

gently but firmly taking Evelyn's arm. "We must go. Now."

With a gentle tug, Maggie began guiding Evelyn away from the door. Evelyn found herself complying, her feet moving almost of their own accord. As they retreated down the corridor, she cast one last, lingering look over her shoulder at the imposing door.

What secrets are you hiding, Bloodworth Manor? Evelyn thought, a mix of dread and determination settling in her chest. *And why does everyone seem so desperate to keep me from discovering them?*

The sound of their footsteps echoed off the stone walls as they made their way back through the wing, towards the familiar parts of the manor, leaving behind the forbidden wing and its mysteries—for the time being, at least.

The moonlight cast eerie shadows across Evelyn's bedchamber as she tossed and turned, her mind a tempest of unanswered questions. Sleep eluded her, each attempt to close her eyes only bringing visions of that wing and the locked door, and Maggie's fear-stricken face.

"What could possibly be behind that door?" Evelyn whispered to herself, her emerald eyes fixed on the ornate ceiling above. Her fingers absently traced the intricate embroidery of her silk nightgown, a stark reminder of the opulence that now surrounded her, so different from her modest upbringing.

She sat up abruptly, pushing her auburn hair

away from her face. Evelyn swung her legs over the side of the bed, her bare feet meeting the cold floor. She padded to the window, gazing out at the moonlit grounds of Bloodworth Manor. The sprawling estate loomed ominously in the night.

"What am I to do?" she whispered, her breath fogging the glass. "I cannot simply ignore what I've seen, what I've felt."

As if in response to her inner turmoil, exhaustion finally began to overtake her. Evelyn made her way back to bed, her steps heavy with the weight of her thoughts. As she drifted off to sleep, her last conscious thought was of that forbidden wing, calling to her like a siren's song.

In her dreams, Evelyn found herself once again standing in the shadowy corridor of the forbidden wing. The air hung heavy around her, thick with an oppressive silence that seemed to press against her eardrums. Each step she took echoed unnaturally loud, as if the very walls were amplifying her presence.

"Hello?" she called out, her voice sounding small and afraid in the vastness of the corridor. "Is anyone there?"

As if in response, a distant scream pierced the silence, sending chills down Evelyn's spine. It was a sound of pure anguish, reverberating through the halls and growing louder with each passing moment.

"Who's there?" Evelyn cried out, her heart racing as she spun around, trying to locate the source of the terrible sound. "Where are you?"

The screams intensified, seeming to come from everywhere and nowhere at once. Evelyn's breath came in short, panicked gasps as she stumbled forward, drawn inexorably towards the locked door at the end of the forbidden wing.

"I'm coming!" she shouted, her voice trembling with a mix of fear and determination. "Hold on, I'll help you!"

But even as she reached for the door handle, a part of her wondered if she was walking into a trap, sealing her own fate in this nightmare of Bloodworth Manor.

Evelyn's fingers trembled as they grazed the icy surface of the door handle. The metal seemed to pulse beneath her touch, its coldness seeping into her bones. The screams crescendoed, becoming a cacophony of terror that threatened to shatter her resolve.

"I must know," she whispered in her aloud in her sleep, her dream eyes wide with a mixture of fear and determination. "Whatever lies beyond, I cannot turn back now."

As she tightened her grip on the handle, Evelyn noticed something horrifying. The ornate red ivy that adorned the manor's walls began to move, writhing and pulsating like living veins. It oozed a thick, crimson liquid that trickled down the stone walls, pooling at her feet. Like snakes melting over her body as she touched them.

"Dear God," Evelyn gasped, her voice barely

audible over the screams. "What manner of evil is this?"

The blood-like substance crept towards her, staining the hem of her nightgown. Evelyn's heart hammered in her chest, threatening to burst from the confines of her ribcage. With a surge of courage born of desperation, she wrenched the door handle, prepared to face whatever horrors awaited her.

In that instant, Evelyn's eyes flew open. She bolted upright in her bed, her body drenched in a cold sweat. Her chest heaved as she gulped in great lungfuls of air, trying to dispel the lingering terror of her nightmare.

"It was just a dream," she panted, running a trembling hand through her sweat-soaked hair. "Just a dream..."

But even as she spoke the words, Evelyn knew in her heart that it was more than a simple nightmare. The vivid sensations, the palpable fear —it all felt too real, too significant to dismiss.

Evelyn clutched her duvet, her knuckles white as she stared into the darkness of her bedchamber. The echoes of the screams still reverberated in her mind, mingling with the memory of Maggie's fearful eyes earlier that day.

"What are you hiding, Lord Bloodworth?" she whispered, her voice tinged with a mix of anger and apprehension.

As if in response, a floorboard creaked outside her room. Evelyn's breath caught in her throat.

She strained her ears, listening for any sign of movement.

"Is someone there?" she called out, her voice steadier than she felt.

Silence answered her. After a moment, Evelyn swung her legs over the side of the bed, her bare feet touching the cold floor once more, sending a shiver up her spine. She padded to the door and opened it, peering into the hallway.

Empty. The corridor stretched out before her, moonlight casting eerie shadows through the windows.

Evelyn closed the door and leaned against it, her mind racing. Closing the door, she crossed the room to her window. The grounds of Bloodworth Manor lay bathed in silvery moonlight, the manicured gardens a stark contrast to the foreboding woods beyond.

Chapter 5

A Glimmer of Hope

The next three years passed as if in a dream; or, perhaps, more accurately, in a floating state of Purgatory. The seasons drifted by in a blur: winter snow buried secrets and hardships below its white cover as the blood-red ivy twinkled with frost; the fresh dew of spring clung to the grass each year as if by appointment; the summer sun illuminated the world in a way that all thought lost before it reared its scorching head once more; and the autumnal rain dampened the brown leaves that piled up below the many trees surrounding the estate.

Evelyn watched from her perch beside the window, ever aware of the hard surface of the polished mahogany digging into her back, scraping against her bones even through the layers of her dress, her swollen abdomen weighing down upon her hips. She looked dully down at the striped grass of the manor's grand gardens, tracing them as they faded away into the morning mist, stretching out over a sea of grey infinity. The small brick building of the groundkeeper's store was half engulfed by the plague of fog that was creeping over the Bloodworth estate, closer and closer toward the stones that structured this great house, soon to reach the crimson ivy that crawled along the walls. Her noble prison. And as her eyes followed the swirling skies, she found herself envious of the sinking trees, of the gravel pathways, of the beds of tulip touch. Placing a hand upon her expanding waistline, she felt the flutters of the life within, and sighed.

She was envious that the grounds got to disappear, to slink into the ether, whilst she was stuck behind this glass barrier, longing to know the world outwith.

It was as if, with every step she'd taken through the halls of the grand estate, it was a step farther away from the real world, and she couldn't shake the sense of unease that lingered within her soul, every move witnessed by guests and the eyes of strangers, dictated by the whims of her husband.

The weight of her burden seemed to grow heavier with each passing day, a constant reminder of the sacrifices she'd made in the name of duty and obligation. Though she had longed for the bliss of motherhood, Evelyn found herself consumed by a sense of apprehension as news of her pregnancy spread throughout the household. For, despite her husband's occasional requests for her to join His bedchamber, their union remained devoid of passion or intimacy, leaving Evelyn to simply accept the nature of her confinement.

With the passing days stretching into weeks, months, years, Evelyn's emotions became increasingly numb, her heart shielded behind a façade of stoicism and resolve. She had resigned herself to her fate, accepting the reality of her situation with a sense of passive acceptance. Yet, amidst the opulence of the manor and the trappings of her privileged existence, Evelyn couldn't shake the feeling of emptiness that gnawed at her soul, a silent reminder of the price she had paid for her position as the lady of the house.

As Shakespeare once wrote, 'expectation is the root of all heartache.'

And now, every time she felt the movement within her, she couldn't help but fear what lay ahead, not only for her, but for her child.

She looked down at the volume in her hand and gently lifted it to her nose, inhaling the scents of the world held within its delicate pages. She found she could never quite explain the simple pleasure in the smell of books, but it was something that comforted her greatly.

The world outside the window seemed to fade away as she delved into the pages of 'The Voyage Out', her mind transported to the vivid landscapes and intricate characters Woolf had so masterfully crafted.

As she read, Evelyn felt herself slipping into the narrative, her own troubles momentarily forgotten in the face of Rachel Vinrace's journey of self-discovery. The protagonist's quest for meaning and identity resonated deeply with Evelyn, mirroring her own silent struggles within the confines of her gilded cage. The lyrical prose and Woolf's keen insights into the human condition offered Evelyn a semblance of companionship, a reminder that she was not entirely alone in her yearning for freedom and understanding.

The afternoon light cast a golden glow across the pages of the book, and Evelyn allowed herself to be completely absorbed by the story. In those precious moments, the weight of her reality lifted, replaced by the liberating power of the words in front of her. And as she turned each page, Evelyn found a flicker of hope rekindled within her heart, a reminder that even in the darkest of times, the written word held the power to illuminate and inspire.

"My lady?" The sound of Florence's voice almost made her jump, pulling her back to reality.

"Florence," Evelyn sighed, placing her book down upon her lap and smiling up at the girl, "are you all right?"

"Sorry to disturb you, my lady, but a letter has arrived for you," the housemaid smiled gingerly and offered the correspondence from her hand.

With a mixture of curiosity and trepidation,

Evelyn set aside her book and reached for the letter. As she unfolded the crisp paper, her emerald eyes darted across the elegant script:

My dearest Lady Bloodworth,

I hope this letter finds you well. I write to inform you that I, Archibald Bates, cousin to your esteemed husband, will be arriving at Bloodworth Manor in a fortnight's time for a familial visit...

Evelyn's breath caught in her throat. Archibald Bates—the name conjured a fleeting memory of twinkling eyes and an easy smile from her wedding day, a stark contrast to the austere faces of the Bloodworth family.

"Oh my," she murmured, her hand absently coming to rest on the swell of her belly. "I wonder whatever for."

As she continued reading, a myriad of emotions flitted across her face—curiosity, apprehension, and a hint of something that might have been hope, had it not been so long that she barely remembered what it felt like.

Yours truly,

Archie

Evelyn folded the letter carefully, her thoughts a whirlwind. "Archie Bates," she whispered to herself, "I wonder what sort of man you've become."

The fortnight passed in a blur of anticipation and

preparation. On the morning of Archie's arrival, Evelyn stood by the grand staircase, watching the flurry of activity below. Maids scurried about with fresh linens, footmen polished every surface of each floor to a mirror shine, and the air was thick with the scent of beeswax and lemon.

"My lady," Maggie, the housekeeper, approached with a curtsy, followed closely by Florence. "I was wondering if you'd given any thought as to the menu for tonight's function?"

Evelyn sighed heavily; her husband may be renowned for His many extravagant dinners and balls, but it would seem that no one thought to question who might be the true organiser behind such occasions. For if they thought it was the Marquis Himself, then they would be sorely mistaken.

"Yes, of course, sorry," Evelyn rubbed her eyes with her index finger and thumb. "I'm thinking for the hors d'oeuvres we should have a selection of devilled eggs and canapés. Oh! And do be sure to include ham and cheese sandwiches, cut into triangles, if that's all right."

"Of course, ma'am. And for the main course?"

"I'd like it if we go for lamb, given that there will be some foreign dignitaries in attendance. Probably best if it comes from one of the local farms, that way it gives the Marquis an excuse to brag about the local countryside to anyone who cares to listen."

Florence stifled a giggle and briefly lifted a hand to cover her girlish grin at how open she found the Lady to be in her presence. Since their first meeting, the young housemaid had found herself to be ever so comfortable in the presence of her new boss, as she chimed in. "Any dessert ideas, ma'am?"

"Perhaps just red velvets and pound cakes. I don't want to put too much pressure on the kitchen. Especially considering that I have no idea what this particular function is even for. Other than the arrival of Mr. Bates—though, Lord Bloodworth has never shown this amount of care for him before."

As Florence hid her giggles once again—though rather poorly—Evelyn simply smiled back at her, wishing her life were not this repeated monotony of functions and balls that seemed to mean quite so little to her. An endless stream of strangers seemed to enter her life with no purpose she could ever quite envision. Giving a small curtsy, the housemaid and -keeper bowed their heads slightly and made their exits from the room, leaving Evelyn alone once more, her attention once again wandering back to staring at the world outside the window.

Once the evening quickly came around, as they all seemed to do, nobody could deny that the function hall looked incredible, as it always did. The multiple round tables were covered in the finest ruby cloths; the red roses bunched around the room in various old and impressive vases; and the gilded chairs (that looked ever so uncomfortable) matched perfectly with the frames of the ever so imposing ancestral portraits that seemed to line every corner and crevice, perpetually reminding Evelyn just how alien she was in her own home.

She washed her eyes over the room of guests, some of whom she recognised from previous engagements she'd hosted, some of whom were perfect strangers; none of them with names she could ever remember. She wondered as she looked around and nodded congenially at each guest if any of them could see the emptiness in her eyes, the sparkle that once used to live there dampened to nothingness in the years she'd spent being Lady Bloodworth.

Then, as she stood there with a glass of wine in hand, she felt it again. That flutter deep within her abdomen that still made her gasp every time. And, in that moment, she felt something. Something that twisted her insides; something that she could never quite name; something that reminded her that she existed.

"Evelyn!" She almost jumped as she heard His voice. Not His real voice, not the dominating cruelty and cold she heard around their house, but the one He used in front of guests; the one that made Him sound almost as if He cared. Almost as if He wasn't fucking every housemaid and whore who'd have Him. "Evelyn, darling! Do come here, I have someone for you to meet!"

She took a deep breath, put on her best smile, and made her way over toward her husband and the small group of people gathered around Him. She nodded congenially at the guests bunched around Him as she approached, bracing herself for another long and draining story about something she didn't care to understand. Evelyn found herself to be entirely correct as she was introduced to three or four faces she was sure would barely register in her brain.

Evelyn offered a small smile. "Yes, Maggie. The staff have outdone themselves."

"We were all quite excited for Mr. Bates' arrival," Maggie confided, her eyes twinkling. "It's been so long since we've had a proper visitor."

Evelyn nodded, feeling a pang of loneliness. "Indeed, it has."

As Maggie bustled away, Evelyn's hand came to rest on her belly once more. "Well, little one," she murmured, "it seems we're about to have some company. I do hope you'll behave yourself."

She watched as a maid nearly toppled a vase in her haste, only to be steadied by a footman. Their shared laugh echoed through the hall; a sound so rare in these austere walls that it made Evelyn's heart ache.

The crunch of gravel announced the arrival of the carriage, and Evelyn's chest quickened despite her efforts to remain composed. As the footmen rushed to attend to the vehicle, a figure emerged with an energetic leap, his fair hair catching the sunlight where he stood.

Archie Bates' easy smile was immediately apparent as he greeted the staff, shaking hands and offering warm words that elicited genuine laughter. Evelyn observed from her position near the entrance, struck by the stark contrast between Archie's demeanour and the usual somber atmosphere of Bloodworth Manor.

"James, my good man! Still keeping everyone in line, I see," Archie's voice carried, filled with warmth and mirth. He turned, his gaze finding Evelyn, and for a moment, she felt exposed under his keen observation.

Evelyn's breath caught as she truly saw him for the first time since her wedding. Gone was the vague memory of a distant relation, the young man he had once been—the youths they had both been; in its place stood a man whose presence seemed to brighten the very air around him.

"Lady Bloodworth," Archie approached with a large grin, bowing with a flourish that somehow managed to be both respectful and playful all at once. "It's a pleasure to see you again. I trust you're well?"

Evelyn inclined her head, her voice carefully modulated as she replied, "Welcome to Bloodworth Manor, Mr. Bates. I hope your journey was pleasant."

As they moved to the drawing room, Evelyn found herself acutely aware of Archie's proximity. His scent, a blend of sandalwood and something uniquely him, which she seemed still to remember after these three years, wafted gently, a stark contrast to the Marquis' overpowering cologne, imported (expensively, as he'd always remind her) from France.

Once seated, Archie leaned forward, his eyes twinkling. "I must say, Lady Bloodworth, you're looking radiant. Motherhood clearly agrees with you."

Evelyn felt a blush creep up her neck. "You're too kind, Mr. Bates. And please, call me Evelyn. We are family, after all."

"Only if you'll call me Archie," he replied with a grin. "Mr. Bates makes me feel like a stuffy old man, and I'd like to think I'm far from that. Not quite approaching that hill, not quite yet."

A small smile tugged at Evelyn's lips, remembering just how much closer they were in age. "Very well... Archie."

Evelyn found herself relaxing incrementally. Archie's genuine warmth was disarming.

As the afternoon light filtered through the library's tall windows, Evelyn's fingers found themselves again tracing the spine of the leather-bound volume she'd found herself abandoning over the previous two weeks. A part of her almost felt sad, like in the whirlwind of getting everything organised for new company, she'd forgotten an old friend.

"Ah, Woolf," he remarked, while absently plucking another book from a shelf just down from where she stood. "A favourite of yours, I presume?"

Evelyn's eyes widened slightly. "Indeed. How did you know?"

Archie's lips quirked into a mischievous smile. "Elementary, my dear Evelyn. The well-worn edges speak volumes, if you'll pardon the pun."

A small laugh escaped her, surprising even herself. "I see your wit is as sharp as ever, Mr. Bates. Though I confess, I didn't expect you to be an admirer of such novels."

"Oh, but I am full of surprises," he replied, his tone light yet tinged with something deeper. "Like Elizabeth Bennet, I dearly love to laugh. And, as I dare remind the Lady of the house, it's Archie. But, my Lady Bloodworth, forgive give me, but may I ask, pray tell, why it is you spend so many long hours with your nose in a book?"

"Why, Mr. Bates? Are you of the persuasion that women should not be educated?"

"Of course not, not at all. For that claim would be at once absurd and unsubstantial. It was simply a wondering, that is all."

Evelyn felt a spark of intellectual curiosity ignite within her. "And what of Mr. Darcy? Do you find his character as compelling as many do?"

"Compelling, yes, but perhaps in need of a good shake," Archie mused, settling into a nearby armchair. "Though I suppose we all have our pride to contend with."

As they delved deeper into literary discourse, Evelyn found herself becoming more animated, her usual reserve giving way to genuine enthusiasm. Archie listened intently; his eyes alight with interest as Evelyn expounded on her analysis of Austin and Woolf's prose. She found herself gesturing more freely, her voice gaining strength as she shared her thoughts on the symbolism and themes woven throughout the novel.

"You know," Archie said, leaning forward, "I believe there's more of Elizabeth in you than you realise, Evelyn."

She raised an eyebrow. "How so?"

"That fire in your eyes when you speak of something you're passionate about. It's quite captivating."

Evelyn felt a warmth spread through her chest, not entirely due to her condition. "I... thank you, Archie. It's been some time since I've had the opportunity for such stimulating conversation."

A shadow of concern flickered across Archie's face, but before he could respond, the gentle chimes of a clock interrupted.

"Oh," Evelyn exclaimed, rising carefully. "I hadn't realised the time. Shall we adjourn to the music room? I believe tea will be served there shortly, and I cannot abide the hustle and bustle of the affair taking place in the function room."

As they entered the sun-drenched chamber, Archie's gaze fell upon the grand piano and he gestured toward it. "Do you play?"

She hesitated, her hand unconsciously moving to her swollen belly, and her mind moving much farther back. "I... used to. It's been some time."

"Would you indulge me with a piece?" Archie asked, his voice gentle and encouraging; not cold and forceful, as she'd become so used to in the past three years.

Evelyn wavered, torn between desire and apprehension. "I'm not sure I remember how," she admitted softly.

"Nonsense," Archie said, guiding her to the bench. "Music isn't something you forget. It's something that lives in your soul."

With a deep breath, Evelyn took a seat and placed her fingers on the keys. The first notes were tentative, halting, but as the melody took shape, she felt a familiar warmth spread through her. Chopin' Nocturne in E-flat major filled the room, her confidence growing with each measure.

Suddenly, she felt a flutter within her womb, more pronounced than ever before. Her playing faltered for a moment as she gasped softly.

"Evelyn?" Archie's voice was laced with concern. "Are you all right?"

A radiant smile bloomed on her face, and she couldn't help but let loose a soft laugh. "Yes, I... the baby. It's moving. Dancing, almost."

Archie's eyes lit up with wonder. "Well then, by all means, don't stop on my account. It seems we have an appreciative audience."

As Evelyn resumed playing, her heart swelled with a joy she hadn't felt in years. For a brief, shining moment, the oppressive weight of Bloodworth Manor seemed to lift, replaced by the sweet harmony of music and new life.

It was some time after lunch that Evelyn found herself inhaling the gentle fragrance of roses that wafted through the air as she and Archie strolled along the winding garden path. Sunlight dappled the ground through the leaves of ancient oaks, creating a tranquil tapestry that stood in stark contrast to the looming presence of Bloodworth Manor behind them.

Evelyn's hand rested lightly on Archie's arm, her emerald eyes taking in the vibrant blooms surrounding them. She inhaled deeply, savouring the momentary respite from the suffocating atmosphere within the manor walls.

"I must say, Lady Bloodworth," Archie began, his voice warm and tinged with concern, "these gardens are a veritable paradise. Though I can't help but notice that you seem... weighed down by something. Are you feeling quite well?"

Evelyn's steps faltered slightly, her heart quickening. She struggled internally, weighing the risk of revealing too much against her desperate need for understanding.

"I... I'm managing, thank you," she replied carefully, her tone measured. "The pregnancy has been... challenging at times."

Archie's brow furrowed as he studied her face. "Is there anything I can do to help? Anything you need?"

Evelyn felt a lump form in her throat, touched by his genuine concern. "You're very kind, but I—" She paused, gathering her courage. "The truth is,

Archie, this place can be... overwhelming."

"How so?" he prodded gently.

She sighed, her eyes clouding with a mixture of sadness and resignation. "It's as if, sometimes, I find myself sitting there, and the very walls of the manor seem to close in around me..."

Archie's hand covered hers reassuringly. "My dear Evelyn, you mustn't blame yourself. I spent a great deal of my childhood here..." He trailed off before taking a breath. "And this place would dampen anyone's spirits. But you're carrying new life—that's a miraculous thing."

Evelyn managed a small smile, grateful for his understanding. "Thank you, Archie. Your kindness means more than you know."

As they continued their walk, Evelyn felt a tiny weight lift from her shoulders. Though she had revealed only a fraction of her discontent, the simple act of sharing had provided a glimmer of solace in her otherwise lonely world.

The following days saw Evelyn and Archie gravitating towards each other, their interactions becoming more frequent and natural. One afternoon, they again found themselves in the library, surrounded by towering shelves of leather-bound books.

"Have you read this one lately?" Archie asked, pulling out a well-worn volume of Austen's *Pride and Prejudice.*

Evelyn's eyes lit up. "Oh, yes. It's one of my favourites. Elizabeth Bennet is such a wonderfully spirited character."

Archie chuckled, his blue eyes twinkling. "I knew you'd have understood our conversation, and she reminds me a bit of you, actually."

A faint blush crept across Evelyn's cheeks. "Yes, you've said. But I'm afraid I'm not nearly as clever or outspoken."

"I beg to differ," Archie countered, leaning against a bookshelf. "You have a quiet strength about you, Evelyn. It's quite captivating."

Evelyn felt a flutter in her chest, both thrilled and unnerved by his words. She absently placed a hand on her abdomen, feeling the baby shift beneath her touch.

"Speaking of strength," Archie said softly, noticing her gesture. "How are you feeling today?"

"Better than I have in a while," Evelyn admitted, surprised to find it was true. "Your presence has brought a certain... lightness to the manor."

Archie's smile widened. "I'm glad to hear it. Perhaps we could make this a regular occurrence? Reading together, I mean."

Evelyn nodded, a genuine smile gracing her features. "I'd like that very much."

Later that evening, alone in her chambers, Evelyn stood before her mirror, studying her reflection. Her hands cradled her belly, a mix of emotions swirling within her.

"Little one," she whispered, her voice trembling slightly. "I can't wait to meet you, to hold you in my arms. But I'm so afraid..." She closed her eyes, memories of Julien's cold indifference washing over her.

It was only a week later when the searing pain tore through Evelyn's body, ripping a primal scream from her throat. The midwife's urgent voice piercing through the haze of agony.

"Push, milady! Push!"

Evelyn bore down, her fingers clawing at the sweat-soaked sheets. The metallic scent of blood filled her nostrils as another contraction wracked her frame.

"I... can't," she gasped, tears streaming down her flushed cheeks. "I can't do this."

The midwife's weathered hand grasped hers. "You can, Lady Bloodworth. Your baby needs you to be strong."

Evelyn's eyes flashed with determination. With a guttural cry, she summoned every ounce of strength left in her exhausted body and pushed.

But as it happened, there He stood at the end of the room, watching it all before Him, as if it were paramount only to His life, to His wellbeing, not hers.

And in a matter of minutes He watched as it changed. That soft, wet cunt, the very one whose innocence He'd penetrated Himself, was suddenly sullied in His eyes. The days when He'd first hunted its supple skin, first hungered for its fresh flesh, now seemed an eternity behind Him. The seal He'd broken, the wound He'd first made bleed, had now been replaced by this vulgar cavern. It had split wide open, no longer a tool for His arousal, but an opening into the unknown depths of the tombs from whence man came. A tunnel to the centre of the Earth, to the centre of all life, to the secret of what makes man, man. And it disgusted Him.

Moments later, a tiny, indignant wail filled the room.

"He's here," the midwife announced, her voice thick with emotion. "Your son, milady, my lord, your son!"

Evelyn collapsed against the pillows, her chest heaving. "Let me see him," she whispered.

The midwife placed the squalling bundle in her arms. Evelyn gazed down at her son's scrunched face, overwhelmed by a love so fierce it took her breath away.

"Edgar," she murmured, tracing his tiny features

with trembling fingers. "My beautiful boy."

As she cradled him close, Evelyn's voice dropped to a fierce whisper. "I will never let anyone hurt you, my darling. I swear it."

The door creaked open, and Julien's imposing figure left the threshold.

Evelyn felt a familiar sting of shame. "Edgar, that shall be your name."

As the door closed behind him, Evelyn looked down at Edgar's peaceful face. "We'll be all right, my love," she whispered, a newfound resolve settling over her like armour. "You've given me a strength I never knew I possessed."

Evelyn gazed at her son; his tiny fingers curled around her thumb. The weight of him in her arms anchored her to this moment, to this new reality that had blossomed in the wake of his birth. Sunlight streamed through the window, casting a warm glow over them both as they lay there in the birthing bed.

"You've changed everything, my darling," she murmured, tracing the curve of his cheek with a gentle finger. "I never knew I could love someone so fiercely, so completely."

Edgar stirred, his dark green eyes—so like her own—blinking open. Evelyn's heart swelled with an emotion so profound it bordered on pain.

"What do you think of this grand old house,

hmm?" she asked, her voice soft. "It may seem cold now, but I promise you, we'll fill it with warmth and laughter. Someday. Somehow. I promise you."

A few hours later, when they'd both had some time to rest together, she rose carefully from the bed, cradling Edgar close as she moved to the window. The vast Bloodworth estate stretched out before them, a world of possibility and peril.

"There's so much I want to show you, to teach you," Evelyn said, her tone growing determined. "But, most importantly, I want you to know love. Real love, not the hollow imitation that haunts these halls."

Edgar cooed softly, and Evelyn felt a surge of protective instinct course through her.

"Your father may be disappointed in me, in us, perhaps," she whispered, "but I won't let that define us. We're going to forge our own path, you and I."

She turned from the window, her posture straightening as a newfound resolve settled over her.

"I may have entered this house as a timid girl, but for you, my love, I'll become the mother you deserve. Strong. Resilient. Unafraid."

Evelyn's eyes shone with determination as she looked down at her son. And in that moment, she felt the first stirrings of resolve in her mind, wanting nothing more than to find a way to secure a future filled with the love and warmth Edgar deserved.

"We have quite the adventure ahead of us," she said, a smile playing at her lips. "And I can't wait to see where it leads."

Chapter 6

The Price of Defiance

The soft melody of Chopin's Nocturne in E-flat major filled the drawing room once more, Evelyn's fingers dancing across the ivory keys with practiced grace. She glanced over her shoulder, a gentle smile playing on her lips as she caught sight of Edgar, peacefully slumbering in the wooden crib they kept in the drawing room—Evelyn liked him to have a crib in all the rooms she spent her days, so he was never too far from her side. The afternoon sun cast a warm glow through the tall windows, bathing the room in golden light.

Evelyn's eyes closed as she lost herself in the music, her body swaying slightly with the rhythm. For a moment, she allowed herself to forget the weight of her responsibilities, the constant tension that permeated throughout Bloodworth Manor.

As the final notes faded, Evelyn rose from

the piano bench, smoothing down her skirts. She approached Edgar's crib, gazing down at her sleeping son with a mixture of love and fierce protectiveness.

"My darling boy," she whispered, her voice barely audible. "I promise you, I will find a way to give you the life you deserve." With a soft sigh, Evelyn quietly left the room, careful not to disturb Edgar's slumber. As she stepped into the hallway, her heart skipped a beat at the sight of Archie approaching from the opposite direction.

"Lady Bloodworth," Archie greeted her, his voice warm and his eyes twinkling with their usual mischief. "I hope I'm not interrupting your afternoon repose."

Evelyn felt a smile tugging at her lips despite herself. "Not at all, Mr. Bates. I was just playing for Edgar. I didn't expect you here."

Archie's expression softened at the mention of the child. "Ah, the young master. How is he faring?"

"He's growing stronger every day," Evelyn replied, unable to keep the pride from her voice, yet noticing how he dodged the question of his current arrival. She hesitated, then added softly, "Your kindness towards him… it means more than you know. I'm sure he loves your visits, even if he is still a little young to have the capacity to verbalise it."

A flicker of something deeper passed through Archie's eyes, and he took a half-step closer. "It's my pleasure, truly. Edgar is a gorgeous child... much like his mother."

Evelyn felt a blush rising to her cheeks, and she lowered her gaze. In her mind, she could hear Julien's cold voice, consistently reminding her of her place. But Archie's presence seemed to push those thoughts away, replacing them with a warmth she hadn't felt in years.

"You're too kind, Mr. Bates," she murmured, forcing herself to maintain a semblance of propriety.

Archie's hand twitched at his side, as if he longed to reach out to her. Instead, he simply inclined his head. "I speak only the truth, Evelyn. Your strength... it's inspiring."

Their eyes met, and for a moment, the air between them seemed charged with unspoken emotions. Evelyn's heart raced, torn between the desire to linger in Archie's presence and the knowledge that she must be cautious.

"I... I should return to Edgar," she said finally, her voice barely above a whisper, forgetting entirely why she had left the room to begin with.

Archie nodded, taking a respectful step back, and gave a slight smile. "Of course. Give the young master my regards."

As Evelyn turned back toward room, she felt Archie's gaze following her. She allowed herself one last glance over her shoulder, catching sight of the longing in his eyes that mirrored her own hidden desires.

With each step back towards the drawing room, Evelyn's resolve strengthened. She would protect her son, navigate the treacherous waters of Bloodworth Manor, and perhaps... just perhaps... find a way to nurture the fragile hope that Archie's presence had awakened in her heart.

From the shadows of a nearby alcove, Julien Bloodworth watched the exchange between his wife and cousin with narrowed eyes, his jaw clenching with barely contained fury. The sight of Evelyn's flushed cheeks and Archie's tender gaze ignited a smouldering rage within him.

"So, the little sparrow thinks she can fly," Julien muttered under his breath, his imposing figure casting a long shadow across the hallway. His hand tightened around the ornate walking stick he carried around these days, knuckles turning white with the force of his grip.

As Evelyn disappeared behind the door once more, Julien emerged from his hiding place, his cold eyes fixed on Archie's retreating form. *I'll clip those wings,* he vowed silently, *and remind her of her cage.*

The dinner bell chimed, its melodious tone a stark contrast to the tension permeating the air. Julien straightened his already impeccable jacket and made his way to the dining room, his footsteps echoing ominously throughout the manor.

Later, as the family gathered around the opulent dining table, Julien sat at its head, his presence looming over the room like a storm cloud. Evelyn could feel his gaze boring into her as she took her seat, her fingers trembling slightly as she arranged her napkin.

"I trust you had a... productive afternoon, my dear," Julien's voice cut through the silence, each word dripping with thinly veiled accusation.

Evelyn's heart raced, but she kept her composure. "Yes, my lord. I spent some time with Edgar in the drawing room. He sleeps so soundly to the piano these days."

"How delightful," Julien replied, his tone devoid of warmth. His eyes slid to Archie, who was busying himself with his soup. "And you, cousin? How did you occupy yourself since your arrival this afternoon? The manor is treating you well, as usual, I presume?"

Archie looked up, his usual charm tempered by caution. "Oh, just exploring the grounds, admiring the gardens, seeing all the new season has to offer. Your estate is truly magnificent, Julien."

"Indeed," Julien said, his lip curling into a sneer. "Though, I wonder if it's the gardens that hold your interest, or perhaps... other attractions."

Evelyn felt her cheeks burn, but she forced herself to meet Julien's gaze. "The soup is excellent tonight, my lord. Perhaps, we could discuss the upcoming harvest festival?"

Julien's eyes flashed dangerously. "Always so eager to change the subject, aren't you, Evelyn? One might think you have something to hide."

As the tension at the table thickened, Evelyn's mind raced. She knew she had to tread carefully, for Edgar's sake as much as her own. But beneath her fear, a quiet determination burned. She would endure, she would protect, and somehow, she would find a way to break free from the suffocating control of Bloodworth Manor... and, more accurately, of Lord Bloodworth himself.

The clock chimed nine, its somber tones echoing through the manor's halls. Julien's voice cut through the air, sharp as a blade. "Evelyn, attend me in my study. Now."

Evelyn's fingers trembled slightly as she placed her napkin beside her plate. She rose, her deep green eyes meeting Julien's steely gaze.

"Of course, my lord," she replied, her voice steady despite the fear coiling in her stomach.

As she followed Julien's imposing figure down the corridor, Evelyn's mind whirled. What new torment awaited her? She steeled herself, drawing strength from thoughts of Edgar's innocent face.

The study door creaked open, and Julien gestured her inside with a curt nod. Evelyn entered, the scent of leather and aged whiskey assaulting her senses.

Julien circled her like a predator, his footsteps heavy on the Persian rug. "Your behaviour of late has been... disappointing, Evelyn," he began, voice low and menacing.

Evelyn stood tall, chin lifted. "I'm not sure I understand, my lord. How have I disappointed you?"

Julien's hand slammed down on his desk, making her flinch. "Don't play coy with me!" he snarled. "I've seen the way you look at Archie, the stolen glances, the hushed conversations."

"Archie is family," Evelyn replied, fighting to keep her voice even. "Surely it's natural to be cordial—"

"Cordial?" Julien interrupted, his face inches from hers. "Is that what you call it? You forget your place, woman. You are my wife, and you will conduct yourself accordingly."

Evelyn's heart pounded, but she met his gaze unflinchingly. "I have never forgotten my place or my duties, Julien. I've given you an heir, I manage your household—"

"Silence!" Julien roared, his hand raised as if to strike. Evelyn braced herself, but the blow didn't fall. Instead, Julien's voice dropped to a deadly whisper. "Remember this, Evelyn. Everything you have—your status, your son, this roof over your head—it all comes from me. And I can take it away just as easily."

Evelyn's breath caught in her throat, her striking eyes widening at Julien's threat. The weight of his words pressed down on her chest, but she refused to let her composure crumble. Her thoughts immediately flew to Edgar, her precious son sleeping peacefully in his nursery, blissfully unaware of the storm raging around him.

"You wouldn't dare," she whispered, her voice barely audible.

Julien's lips curled into a cruel smile. "Wouldn't I? Test me, Evelyn, and you'll see just how far I'm willing to go."

As he turned away, Evelyn's hands clenched at her sides, her nails digging into her palms. She could feel the familiar fire of maternal protection igniting within her, fuelling her resolve.

I will endure, she thought fiercely. *For Edgar, I will endure anything.*

"Is that all, my lord?" she asked, her tone steady despite the tremor in her heart.

Julien waved a dismissive hand. "You may go. And remember, I'll be watching."

Evelyn curtsied stiffly and turned to leave. As she reached for the door handle, she paused, her hand hovering for a moment. *I must find a way,* she vowed silently. *A way to protect us both.*

She stepped into the hallway; her footsteps measured and deliberate on the polished floor. The weight of Julien's threats hung heavy in the air, but with each step, Evelyn felt her determination solidify.

Archie, she thought, her heart constricting. His warmth and kindness had been a balm to her soul, but now... Now she knew she must be cautious. Julien's watchful eyes would miss nothing, and she couldn't risk giving him any reason to act on his threats.

As she made her way back to her chambers, Evelyn's mind raced with plans and possibilities. She would find a way to navigate this treacherous path, to keep her son safe, to preserve the small moments of joy she had found. It wouldn't be easy, but then again, nothing in her life at Bloodworth Manor ever had been.

Evelyn's feet carried her past her chambers, drawn by an invisible thread to the warmth of the kitchen. As she descended the narrow servants' staircase, the oppressive chill of the manor seemed to lift, replaced by the comforting aroma of freshly baked bread and simmering stew.

She paused in the doorway, watching Florence bustling about, her cheerful humming a stark contrast to the sombre mood upstairs. The kitchen glowed with golden lamplight, reflecting off copper pots and well-worn wooden surfaces. It was a haven of simplicity and comfort in a house that often felt more like a prison.

"Oh! Lady Bloodworth," Florence exclaimed, noticing Evelyn. Her kind eyes crinkled with concern. "Is everything alright? You look pale as a ghost."

Evelyn stepped fully into the kitchen, letting the door swing shut behind her. "Florence," she began, her voice barely above a whisper, "I... I need to talk to someone."

Florence immediately set aside the pot she was scrubbing. "Of course, my lady. Here, sit down." She pulled out a chair at the sturdy kitchen table. "Would you like some tea?"

Evelyn nodded gratefully, sinking into the seat. As Florence busied herself with the kettle on the stove, Evelyn's fingers traced the grain of the wooden tabletop, gathering her thoughts.

"It's Julien," she said finally, her voice low and strained. "He... he made threats. About Edgar. About what he'd do if I..." She trailed off, unable to voice the full extent of her husband's menace, or her feelings for Archie.

Florence set a steaming cup before Evelyn, then sat across from her, reaching out to clasp her hand. "Oh, dear," she said softly. "That man... he's a right devil, he is. But you listen to me. You're stronger than he knows. We'll find a way to keep you and little Edgar safe."

Evelyn's eyes glistened with unshed tears. "But how, Florence? He sees everything, controls everything. I feel like I can hardly breathe without his permission."

"Now, now," Florence soothed, her warm hand squeezing Evelyn's. "You've got more allies than you realise. We may be just servants, but we've got eyes and ears all over this house. And not one of us would let any harm come to you or that sweet baby."

A small spark of hope kindled in Evelyn's chest. She took a sip of tea, letting its warmth fortify her. "Thank you, Florence. I don't know what I'd do without you."

As they sat in companionable silence, Evelyn's mind whirled. Perhaps, with Florence's help and the support of the other household staff, she could find a way to navigate the treacherous waters ahead. It wouldn't be easy, but she was no longer the timid girl who had first arrived at Bloodworth Manor. She was a mother now, with a fierce determination to protect her child at all costs.

I will find a way, she vowed silently, her grip tightening on the teacup. *For Edgar's sake, and for my own.*

Florence's kind eyes sparkled as she leaned in, her voice barely above a whisper. "My lady, I've been in this house for most of my life. I've seen the darkness that lurks in its corners, but I've also seen light prevail. We'll be your eyes and ears, Evelyn. You're not alone in this."

Evelyn's heart swelled with gratitude. "Oh, Florence," she breathed, reaching out to clasp the young woman's hands. "I don't know how to thank you."

"Hush now," Florence replied, a determined glint in her eye. "You just focus on keeping yourself and that precious boy of yours safe. Leave the rest to us."

As Evelyn rose to leave, Florence took a small vial out of her robes and pressed it into her palm. "Lavender oil," she explained. "For peaceful sleep. You'll need your strength."

Evelyn nodded, tucking the vial into her pocket. She made her way through the shadowy corridors, her footsteps echoing in the oppressive silence. Her mind raced, replaying Julien's threats and Florence's promises in equal measure.

Entering her chambers, Evelyn's gaze immediately fell on the crib of Edgar's that lived in her room. She approached it silently, watching her son's peaceful slumber. *I will be strong for you, my love,* she thought, gently stroking his soft, pink cheek. *No matter what your father does, I will find a way to keep you safe.*

Evelyn turned from Edgar's crib; her rich green eyes drawn to the expansive window that dominated one wall of her chamber. She moved towards it, her fingers trailing along the cool glass as she gazed out at the moonlit grounds of the Bloodworth estate. The silvery light bathed the manicured gardens and ancient trees in an ethereal glow, a stark contrast to the darkness that seemed to permeate the very walls of the house.

Her reflection stared back at her, a ghost-like figure against the night sky. Evelyn straightened her posture, lifting her chin slightly. "I am Evelyn Appleby, the Lady Bloodworth," she whispered to herself, her voice barely audible. "I will not be broken."

The enormity of her situation threatened to overwhelm her, but Evelyn closed her eyes, drawing a deep breath. When she opened them again, thought back on Edgar's sleeping form behind her. A warmth blossomed in her chest, pushing back against the chill of fear.

"My darling boy," she murmured, her thoughts turning inward. "You give me strength I never knew I possessed. For you, I would move mountains."

A gentle breeze rustled the leaves outside, and Evelyn's mind raced with possibilities. She pressed her palm flat against the windowpane, her voice low but filled with newfound determination. "There must be a way out of this gilded cage. A path to freedom, for both of us."

She turned back to face her sleeping son, a glimmer of hope igniting in her eyes. *I promise you, Edgar,* Evelyn vowed silently, her heart swelling with love and resolve. *We will find that path, no matter how long it takes or how difficult the journey. This is not the end of our story, my love. It's only the beginning.*

As the moon continued its arc across the night sky, Evelyn allowed herself a small, defiant smile. The road ahead would be fraught with danger, but for the first time since arriving at Bloodworth Manor, she felt a flicker of true hope. Whatever challenges lay ahead, she would face them with the quiet strength of a mother's love—a force more powerful than any that Julien could wield against her.

Chapter 7

Whispers of the Heart

The crackling fire cast flickering shadows across the library's mahogany shelves as Evelyn leaned forward in her armchair, captivated by Archie's words. His tousled fair hair caught the warm light, giving him an almost ethereal glow.

"And there I was," Archie said, gesturing animatedly, "face-to-face with a Bengal tiger in the jungles of India. I swear, Evelyn, I could see my reflection in its eyes."

Evelyn's breath caught in her throat. "How terrifying that must have been," she murmured, her deep green eyes wide with fascination.

Archie's lips quirked into a roguish grin. "Terrifying, yes, but exhilarating, too. It's moments like those that make you feel truly alive."

As he spoke, Evelyn found herself leaning closer, drawn in by the passion in his voice. How different he was from Julien, whose words were always measured and cold.

"You must have seen so many wondrous things in your travels," Evelyn said softly. "I can scarcely imagine a world beyond these walls, sometimes."

Archie's expression softened, his eyes meeting hers with gentle understanding. "Perhaps, one day, you'll see it all for yourself, my dear Evelyn. The world has so much beauty to offer."

Evelyn's heart fluttered at the thought. It felt like a long time since she'd seen beauty in the world. As much as she was perfectly aware that she'd never live such a life, never have such adventures as these. But it was nice to pretend. She glanced away, her gaze falling on the window. Dark clouds had gathered on the horizon, and a light drizzle was beginning to fall.

"It seems a storm is brewing," she observed, watching as raindrops began to patter against the glass.

Archie followed her gaze, his voice lowering to match the intimacy of the moment. "All the better for storytelling, wouldn't you agree? There's something rather cozy about being tucked away while the world rages outside."

Evelyn nodded, acutely aware of how secluded they were in that moment. The rain intensified, muffling the sounds of the manor beyond the library doors. It was as if they were in a world of their own, just the two of them. It suddenly seemed as if her husband might have been onto more than even she was aware of.

She turned back to Archie, finding his eyes still on her. A warmth bloomed in her chest, both thrilling and terrifying.

What am I doing? she thought, even as she found herself asking, "Tell me more about your adventures, Archie. I want to hear everything."

Archie leaned forward, his voice dropping to a conspiratorial whisper. "Have I told you about the time I stumbled upon a hidden tomb in Egypt?" His eyes sparkled with mischief and excitement.

Evelyn found herself mirroring his posture, drawn in by the allure of his tale. "No, pray tell," she breathed, her eyes wide with curiosity.

"It was a sweltering day in the Valley of the Kings," Archie began, his words painting vivid pictures in Evelyn's mind. "The air was thick with dust and mystery. I'd wandered off the beaten path, you see, when I noticed an unusual rock formation..."

As Archie's story unfolded, Evelyn's heart raced. She could almost feel the scorching Egyptian sun on her skin, taste the gritty sand in her mouth. Her imagination soared beyond the confines of Bloodworth Manor, to a world of adventure and discovery she'd only ever found in dreams and the words of the greats.

"...and there it was, a chamber untouched for millennia," Archie concluded, his voice filled with wonder.

"How thrilling," Evelyn whispered, her cheeks flushed with excitement. "To uncover such secrets, to be the first to see such marvels in ages. It must be... intoxicating."

A particularly loud crack of thunder made Evelyn jump, startling her from her reverie. The rain was now lashing against the windows with increased ferocity.

Archie glanced towards the tempest outside, then back at Evelyn with a warm smile. "I have an idea," he said, rising from his seat. "Why don't we continue our conversation in the conservatory? The sound of rain on glass is quite soothing, and we'll have a spectacular view of the storm."

Evelyn hesitated, her sense of propriety warring with her desire to prolong this enchanting interlude.

It wouldn't be proper, a voice in her head cautioned. But another, louder voice whispered of the rare joy she felt in Archie's company.

"I... I suppose that would be lovely," she found herself saying, even as her cheeks coloured at her own daring.

As they made their way to the conservatory, Evelyn's heart pounded. *What am I doing?* she thought.

And yet, she couldn't bring herself to turn back, drawn inexorably forward by Archie's magnetic presence and the promise of more wondrous tales.

The conservatory enveloped them in a verdant embrace, its glass walls streaked with rivulets of rain. Lush ferns and exotic orchids crowded around wrought-iron benches, their leaves glistening in the muted light. The patter of raindrops on the domed ceiling created a soothing rhythm, isolating them from the world beyond.

Evelyn inhaled deeply, the air heavy with the scent of damp earth and blooming jasmine. "It's like stepping into another world," she murmured, trailing her fingers along a vibrant bird of paradise flower.

Archie nodded, his eyes following her movements. "A secret garden, hidden away from prying eyes," he agreed, his voice low and intimate.

They settled onto a bench, closer than propriety dictated, yet not quite touching. The wildness of the foliage seemed to mirror the unruly emotions stirring within Evelyn's breast.

A charged silence fell between them, broken only by the gentle drumming of rain. Evelyn's heart raced, her thoughts a maelstrom of conflicting desires. She stole a glance at Archie, admiring the strong line of his jaw, the warmth in his eyes that so starkly contrasted with Julien's icy stare. Her husband's face swam before her mind's eye—stern, unyielding, a constant reminder of her duty and the gilded cage in which she lived.

"Evelyn," Archie breathed, his gaze intense. "I—"

"Please," she interrupted, her voice trembling. "Don't say it. We mustn't."

But even as the words left her lips, Evelyn felt herself leaning closer, drawn in by an invisible force. She closed her eyes, torn between the sanctity of her marriage vows and the intoxicating promise of Archie's presence.

Archie's hand moved slowly, deliberately, closing the distance between them. His fingers brushed against hers, the touch feather-light, yet electrifying. Evelyn's breath caught in her throat, her emerald eyes widening as she met his gaze.

"I can't help myself," Archie murmured, his voice husky with emotion. "Being near you, Evelyn... it's like basking in the warmth of the sun after a long, cold night."

Evelyn's heart fluttered, a mix of exhilaration and fear coursing through her veins. She knew she should pull away, but found herself unable to move, captivated by the gentle pressure of his hand on hers.

"Archie, we shouldn't," she whispered, even as her fingers intertwined with his. "If anyone were to discover, if Julien—"

A low rumble of thunder cut through her words, reverberating through the conservatory. Archie leaned closer, his eyes never leaving hers.

"I've travelled the world, Evelyn," he said softly, his words filled with sincerity. "I've seen wonders beyond imagination, but nothing compares to the light I see in your eyes. I... I find myself falling for you, more deeply with each passing moment."

Evelyn's breath hitched, her mind reeling. She felt a surge of longing, of possibility, that both thrilled and terrified her.

"Oh, Archie," she breathed, her voice barely audible over the intensifying rain. "I... I don't know what to say. These feelings, they're so..."

She trailed off, torn between the warmth blooming in her chest and the icy grip of apprehension. What would become of her, of her child, if she dared to follow her heart?

The storm outside mirrored the tempest in Evelyn's heart as she gazed into Archie's eyes, finding herself drawn inexorably closer. Lightning flashed, illuminating the lush greenery around them for a breathtaking moment, casting shadows that danced across Archie's handsome features.

"Evelyn," Archie murmured, his voice husky with emotion. "I've never felt this way about anyone before."

She could feel the warmth of his breath on her skin, sending shivers down her spine. Her forest green eyes locked with his, and in that moment, all the unspoken words between them seemed to crystallise into perfect understanding.

"Archie, I..." Evelyn began, her voice trembling. But words failed her as the space between them disappeared.

His smile was just so bright, the flawlessness of the moon shining above them, pouring its light down upon the place where they sat. Evelyn embraced the feeling of blissful chills as he ran his large hands through her hair; gently stroking back her auburn locks, as she looked deeply into his crystalline cerulean eyes. It was paradise, perhaps not exactly in the sense of the word, but it was the closest thing they had.

For he then proceeded to wrap his right arm around her waist, feeling the softness of her curves of her hips press against his strong arms. He continued with his pursuit, and swiftly pulled her into a kiss.

Their lips met, a tingle of pure electricity seeming to run through their bodies, sparking from all around them, losing themselves in this eternal moment. All Evelyn could feel was the warm comfort of his strong arms holding her, keeping her safe from the world outwith. They were all that existed, and everything was absolute. For the first time in years, Evelyn felt as if she knew where she belonged, and it was right here, in his arms, forever.

But the moment didn't last forever, it couldn't,

they were just two star-crossed lovers, kissing in the eye of the storm.

As the kiss deepened, Evelyn's mind raced. *This is wrong,* she thought, even as her body betrayed her, responding to Archie's gentle caress. *I'm a married woman. What would Julien do if he found out? Would he truly be the beast he'd threatened?*

Yet, she couldn't bring herself to pull away, lost in the intoxicating warmth of Archie's embrace. For a fleeting moment, she allowed herself to imagine a life free from the cold confines of her loveless marriage, a life filled with the warmth and affection Archie offered.

But as quickly as it began, the spell was broken. Evelyn's eyes flew open, reality crashing down upon her like a tidal wave. She broke the kiss, her chest heaving as she struggled to catch her breath.

"We... we shouldn't have done that," she whispered, her voice thick with everything she felt all at once.

Evelyn's heart pounded in her chest, her mind a whirlwind of conflicting emotions. The taste of Archie's kiss still lingered on her lips, but it was now tainted with the acrid flavour of guilt. She stepped back, her emerald eyes wide with fear as the full weight of their actions descended upon her.

"If Julien were to find out..." she breathed,

her voice barely audible above the storm raging outside, knowing perfectly well what would happen if he found out. The thought of her husband's icy rage sent a shiver down her spine. "He would be merciless, Archie. Not just to me, but to you, as well..." Her voice broke as she imagined the consequences.

Archie's expression softened, a mixture of regret and longing etched across his handsome features. He reached out as if to touch her cheek but stopped himself, his hand hovering in the air between them.

"Evelyn, I..." he began, his usually confident voice now ting8ed with an air of uncertainness. "I never meant to put you in this position. My feelings for you... they're real, but I understand the impossibility of our situation."

Evelyn closed her eyes, fighting back tears. "We can't, Archie. No matter how much we might want to, we simply can't."

Archie nodded slowly, his tousled hair falling across his forehead. "I know," he said softly. "But I can't help but wonder what life could be like if things were different."

"Please," Evelyn whispered, her resolve wavering. "Don't make this harder than it already is."

With visible effort, Archie took a step back, creating a respectable distance between them. The loss of his proximity left Evelyn feeling both relieved and bereft.

"You're right, of course," he said, his voice thick with emotion. "We have a duty to consider. To your family, to our reputations." He paused, a sad smile playing at the corners of his mouth. "But, know this, Evelyn. My feelings for you won't change, even if we can never act on them."

Evelyn's footsteps echoed through the empty corridors of Bloodworth Manor as she hurried back to her chambers, her heart pounding in her chest. The moment she closed the heavy oak door behind her, she leaned against it, her emerald eyes wide with a mixture of exhilaration and dread.

"What have I done?" she whispered to herself, pushing away from the door and beginning to pace the room. Her fingers trembled as she touched her lips, still tingling from Archie's kiss.

The rain continued to lash against the windows, mirroring the tumultuous emotions raging within her. Evelyn's gaze fell upon her reflection in the ornate mirror, noting the flush in her cheeks and the wild look in her eyes.

"I can't," she muttered, shaking her head. "I mustn't." But even as the words left her mouth, she knew they lacked conviction.

She crossed to the window, pressing her forehead against the cool glass. "Oh, Archie," she sighed, closing her eyes. "Why did you have to make me feel this way?"

The memory of his touch, gentle yet electrifying, sent a shiver down her spine. Evelyn wrapped her arms around herself, torn between the warmth of desire and the chill of fear.

"If Julien were to find out... that his fears had conviction." The thought made her blood run cold. She could almost hear her husband's icy voice, see the cruel glint in his eye. The consequences would be dire, not just for her, but for her child, as well.

Yet, as night fell and Evelyn lay in her bed, sleep eluded her. Every time she closed her eyes, she saw Archie's face, heard his words echoing in her mind.

My feelings for you won't change, he had said, and Evelyn's heart lurched at the memory.

She tossed and turned, the silk sheets tangling around her legs. "What am I to do?" she whispered into the darkness. "How can I choose between duty and... and love?"

The word hung in the air, frightening in its intensity. Evelyn's mind raced with possibilities, each more dangerous than the last. To pursue a relationship with Archie would mean risking everything—her position, her child's future, perhaps even her life.

Yet the alternative—to continue in her loveless marriage to Julien, to deny the passion she felt for

Archie—seemed equally unbearable.

As the first light of dawn crept through the windows, Evelyn remained awake, her eyes fixed on the ceiling. The choices before her loomed large, each path fraught with peril and promise in equal measure.

"Whatever I decide," she murmured, her voice barely audible, "nothing will ever be the same again."

Chapter 8

The Dungeon's Shadow

Evelyn stood at the window; her dark green eyes fixed on the horizon as Archie's carriage disappeared down the long, winding drive of Bloodworth Manor as the afternoon sun began to fade. Her slender fingers pressed against the cold glass, as if reaching for the fleeting happiness that had just slipped away. The late afternoon sun cast long shadows across the manicured grounds, mirroring the darkness creeping back into her heart.

"Goodbye, Archie," she whispered, her breath fogging the windowpane. "Thank you for reminding me what joy feels like."

As the last traces of the carriage vanished from view, Evelyn's shoulders sagged. She turned from the window, her gaze falling on the opulent furnishings of her chambers. The room suddenly felt cavernous, oppressive in its grandeur, as it had so many times before, but this time she could name what it was missing.

"I mustn't give into despair," Evelyn murmured, her voice barely audible. "For Edgar's sake, I must be strong."

She moved to her vanity, studying her reflection in the ornate mirror. The woman staring back at her bore little resemblance to the timid girl who had first arrived at Bloodworth Manor. Her eyes, once wide with innocence, now held a steely determination.

"You've faced worse than this, Evelyn," she told her reflection, straightening her posture. "Archie's visit was a respite, nothing more. Now, you must focus on what truly matters."

The thought of her son, sleeping peacefully in the nursery down the hall, filled Evelyn with renewed purpose. She could almost hear his gentle breathing, feel the warmth of his small body in her arms.

"I won't let this place consume you, my darling," Evelyn vowed, her hands clenching into fists at her sides. "Whatever it takes, I'll find a way to protect you from the shadows that lurk within these walls."

As twilight descended, casting the room in a dusky glow, Evelyn's mind raced with possibilities. Archie's departure had left a void, yes, but it had also ignited a spark of hope. For the first time in years, she dared to imagine a life beyond

Bloodworth Manor.

"Perhaps," she mused, pacing the length of her chambers, "Archie's visit was more than just a fleeting moment of happiness. Perhaps, it was a sign that change is possible."

Evelyn paused; her gaze drawn once more to the window. The grounds below were now shrouded in darkness, but she could still picture the path Archie's carriage had taken. It was a road that led to freedom, to a world beyond the suffocating confines of her gilded cage.

"I may be Lady Bloodworth," she said, her voice gaining strength with each word, "but I am Evelyn Appleby first. And Evelyn Appleby is not afraid to fight for what she loves... for *those* she loves."

With renewed determination, Evelyn moved towards the door. Her son needed her, and she would not let the ghosts of Bloodworth Manor—or its living occupants—stand in her way. As she reached for the handle, a small smile played at the corners of her lips.

"Thank you, Archie," she whispered once more. "You've given me more than you know."

The gas lamps cast flickering shadows along the corridor as Evelyn's footsteps echoed softly against the polished marble floor. She moved with purpose, her emerald eyes alert and scanning the dimly lit passageway. The air grew heavy as she approached the forbidden wing, an invisible barrier that seemed to whisper warnings with each step.

Evelyn's heart quickened, her maternal instincts heightening her senses. *I must be cautious,* she thought, her fingers trailing along the ornate wallpaper. *For Edgar's sake, I cannot afford to be caught here.*

Suddenly, the silence shattered. Raised voices pierced the stillness, sharp and filled with tension. Evelyn froze, recognising the icy timbre of her husband's voice intertwined with Maggie's usually gentle tone.

"You forget your place, woman!" Julien's words cut through the air like a whip. Those words she'd heard so many times directed at herself.

Maggie's response was muffled but defiant. "My lord, I cannot stand by while—"

"Silence!" Julien thundered. "You will do as I command, or you'll find yourself without a position—or worse."

Evelyn's breath caught in her throat. She pressed herself against the wall, her mind racing. *What could have provoked such anger?* she wondered, her curiosity warring with her fear.

The argument continued, hints of power struggles and hidden agendas woven through every heated exchange. Evelyn strained to catch each word, her heart pounding so loudly she feared it might give her away.

Evelyn's heart thundered in her chest as she pressed herself against the cold stone wall, the shadows enveloping her like a protective cloak. She inched closer to the source of the raised voices, her dark green eyes wide with a mix of fear and curiosity.

"You can't keep this up forever, my lord," Maggie's usually soft voice carried an edge of desperation. "The staff are starting to ask questions."

Julien's reply was as sharp as a blade. "The staff will do well to remember their place, as should you, Maggie."

Evelyn's breath caught in her throat. What secrets could be so dire that even loyal Maggie would risk challenging the Marquis?

"But sir, the noises... the screams... The girls seen entering the doors... It's not right, what's happening down there."

A loud thud echoed through the corridor, followed by a whimper. Evelyn's fingers dug into the rough stone, her maternal instincts flaring at the sound of distress.

"You forget yourself," Julien's voice dropped to a dangerous whisper, yet just loud enough for Evelyn to overheard from her hiding place, if she stained hard enough. "Your position here is not guaranteed. One word from me, and you'll find yourself on the streets with nothing but the clothes on your back."

Maggie's reply was barely audible. "Yes, my lord. I... I understand."

"Good. Now get out of my sight."

Evelyn's heart raced as she heard footsteps approaching. She pressed herself further into the shadows, scarcely daring to breathe as Maggie hurried past, her usually neat appearance dishevelled, a red mark blooming on her cheek.

As silence fell over the corridor, the whereabouts of her husband currently unknown as he'd retreated further into his chambers, Evelyn found herself alone, mere steps away from the forbidden wing. Her curiosity warred with her mounting fear, the weight of the manor's secrets pressing down upon her.

What horrors lie beyond that threshold? she wondered, her gaze fixed on the imposing wooden barrier. *And how can I protect my son from whatever evil lurks within these walls?*

With trembling fingers, Evelyn reached out towards the door handle, her resolve strengthening with each passing moment. Whatever lay beyond, she knew she had to uncover the truth—for her sake, and for that of her child.

Evelyn's hand hovered over the ornate doorknob,

her breath shallow and quick. The polished brass felt cold beneath her fingers as she gently pushed, the door creaking open just enough for her to peer inside.

Her eyes widened, adjusting to the gloom. "Oh, merciful heavens," she whispered, her voice barely audible.

The door to a hidden staircase lay stretched open before her, descending into inky darkness. The air that wafted up was damp and chill, carrying with it the faint scent of decay. Evelyn's skin prickled, goosebumps rising along her arms.

She leaned forward, straining to see further into the shadows. "What secrets are you hiding, Julien?" she murmured, her tone a mixture of fear and determination.

Silence enveloped her, broken only by the pounding of her own heart. Then, from the depths below, a sound reached her ears—faint, but unmistakable. A muffled cry, filled with anguish and despair.

Evelyn recoiled, her hand flying to her mouth to stifle a gasp. "Dear God, what manner of evil is this?"

The cry came again, weaker this time, but no less haunting. Evelyn's maternal instincts surged, warring with her self-preservation. She thought of her son, safely tucked away in the nursery, and of the nameless soul suffering in the darkness below.

I cannot stand idly by, she thought to herself, her fingers curling into fists. *But neither can I act rashly. For my child's sake, I must be cautious, yet resolute.*

With a final, shuddering breath, Evelyn stepped back, her mind racing with the implications of her discovery. The manor's sinister secrets were beginning to unravel, and she knew that her life—and the lives of those she held dear—would never be the same.

Evelyn's heart thundered in her chest as she retreated from the forbidden door, her silk slippers barely making a sound on the polished floor. She glanced over her shoulder, half-expecting to see Julien's looming figure, but the corridor remained empty. Her pace quickened, hands trembling as she lifted her skirts to hasten her escape.

I must remain composed, she whispered to herself, forcing her breathing to slow. *For Edgar's sake, I cannot falter now.*

As she rounded the corner towards her chambers, Evelyn nearly collided with Maggie, the housekeeper's eyes widening in surprise.

"My lady! I didn't expect to see you out at this hour," Maggie exclaimed, her gaze darting nervously down the hall.

Evelyn straightened, trying her hardest to ignore the sight of the mark beginning to solidify on the housekeeper's face, to pretend that the dark of the corridor rendered it invisible. "I was merely...

taking a turn about the house. The night air can be so invigorating, don't you agree?"

Maggie's lips thinned. "Indeed, my lady. Though I'd advise against wandering too far. These old houses can be... treacherous in the dark."

"Thank you for your concern, Maggie. I'll keep that in mind."

As Evelyn continued to her room, she could feel Maggie's eyes boring into her back. Once safely inside, she leaned against the door, her mind whirling with questions and fears.

The next morning dawned grey and oppressive. Evelyn moved through the manor, her emerald eyes sharp and observant. The weight of her discovery pressed upon her, lending a new gravity to her movements.

As she walked past the kitchens, she paused, hearing as a scullery maid dropped a plate, shattering the silence. At the abrupt sound, she brushed a stray strand of dark hair behind her ear and entered.

"I'm so sorry, my lady!" the girl cried, her hands shaking as she gathered the broken pieces.

Evelyn knelt beside her. "It's quite alright," she said softly, noting the dark circles under the maid's eyes. "Are you well? You seem... distressed."

The girl's gaze flickered nervously to the cook, who was studiously ignoring them. "I'm fine, my lady. Just... clumsy, is all."

Evelyn helped her to her feet, her touch gentle but her voice firm. "Remember, you can always come to me if you need assistance. With anything."

As she left the kitchen, Evelyn's resolve hardened. The manor's façade of gentility was crumbling, revealing the rot beneath. And she would not rest until she uncovered the truth, no matter the cost.

As Evelyn made her way down the corridor, she spotted a young maid struggling with a heavy tray of tea things. Without hesitation, she approached to lend a hand.

"Here, let me assist you," Evelyn offered, reaching for the tray.

The young girl's eyes widened in surprise. "Oh, my lady, you needn't trouble yourself—"

As their hands met on the tray's edge, Evelyn's gaze caught on the maid's wrists. Angry purple bruises marred the pale skin, partially hidden beneath her sleeves. Evelyn's breath caught in her throat.

"My dear," she said softly, her eyes filled with concern, "what happened to your wrists?"

The young maid quickly pulled her hands away, tugging her sleeves down. "It's nothing, my lady. I... I caught them in a door."

Evelyn's heart raced, her mind flashing to the disturbing sounds she'd heard the night before.

Her brow furrowed. *No-one catches their wrists in a door...*

"Are you certain? You can confide in me if something is amiss."

The young woman's lower lip trembled, her eyes darting nervously. "Please, my lady. I can't... I shouldn't say more."

Evelyn placed a gentle hand on the girl's shoulder. "I understand. But know that you're not alone here. I'm here if you need me."

As the young maid hurried away, Evelyn's thoughts churned with a mix of horror and determination. The bruises were unmistakable evidence of the cruelty lurking within Bloodworth Manor's walls. Her maternal instincts surged, imagining her own child in such a vulnerable position.

"What kind of monster have I married?" she whispered to herself, her fists clenching at her sides. The weight of her situation pressed down upon her, suffocating in its intensity. How could she protect her son in this den of secrets and abuse?

Yet, as the horror of her discovery threatened to overwhelm her, Evelyn felt a steely resolve taking root. She would not cower in the face of this evil. For her child's sake, for the house staff, for her own—she would find a way to fight back.

Evelyn paced her chambers, her green irises darting from object to object as her mind raced. She paused at her writing desk, fingers tracing the ornate patterns on a letter opener.

"I need allies," she murmured, her voice barely above a whisper. "But who can I trust?"

She turned abruptly, her skirts swishing as she moved to her wardrobe. Opening it, she ran her hand along the fine fabrics, considering.

"My jewels," Evelyn thought, her heart quickening. "I could sell them in town, gather funds for our escape."

She shook her head. No, that wouldn't do. She was the Marchioness, they all knew her here, and her husband.

"London," she whispered aloud to herself once more. "I could travel to London and find Archie. I could read over his old letters and find his address. I could…"

Could what? She thought again. *Join another man of the household you're trying to escape? Imagine the Marquis wouldn't simply follow, wouldn't simply come after his child and take him back?*

Evelyn sighed heavily as she felt the tears threaten to fall from her eyes. He'd won. Before she could even try anything, he'd already won.

Chapter 9

A Stolen Summer

The next few years came and went in the blink of an eye. Watching Edgar grow from the small boy she'd held so close to the little toddler running around the manor was a joy like no other, and had been the only thing keeping Evelyn sane.

Then the letter came.

The paper trembled in Evelyn's hands, Archie's familiar scrawl dancing before her eyes. She inhaled sharply, her heart quickening as she absorbed the words.

My dear Evelyn,

I hope this letter finds you well. It is with a heavy heart that I write to inform you of my father's passing. I shall be returning to Bloodworth Manor to sort out the will with Julien. Despite the circumstances, I confess I look forward to seeing you again.

Yours,

Archie

Evelyn pressed the paper to her chest, a storm of emotions swirling within her. "He's coming back," she whispered, her voice a mix of longing and trepidation. "After four years, he's finally coming back."

She paced her chambers, mind racing. *What will I say? How will I act?* She paused at the window, searching the empty driveway. *Oh, Archie, how I've missed you.*

Turning to her wardrobe, Evelyn's fingers brushed across various fabrics before settling on a forest green gown. "This one," she murmured, a faint smile tugging at her lips. "He always said it brought out my eyes."

As she dressed, Evelyn's thoughts wandered. *Will he notice how I've changed? These years have been... challenging.* She smoothed the fabric over her hips, remembering Archie's warm gaze. *But, perhaps, with him here, things might feel lighter again.*

Evelyn returned to the window, her reflection ghostly in the glass. "I shouldn't feel this way," she chided herself. "Julien is my husband, and yet..." She trailed off, watching a bird take flight from a nearby tree. "And yet, with Archie, I feel... free."

A distant rumble caught her attention. Was it thunder, or... ? Evelyn's breath caught as she spotted a carriage in the distance. "He's here," she whispered, her heart hammering against her ribs.

She smoothed her hair, took a steadying breath, and whispered to her reflection, "Be brave, Evelyn. Whatever comes, be brave."

With one last glance at Archie's letter on her dressing table, Evelyn squared her shoulders and left her chambers, each step carrying her closer to a reunion that promised to upend her carefully balanced world.

The crunch of gravel under carriage wheels drew Evelyn to the manor's entrance. Her emerald eyes fixed on the approaching vehicle, heart pounding beneath the green silk. As it came to a halt, Evelyn's breath caught in her throat.

The carriage door swung open, and there he was. Archie Bates, his fair hair tousled by the journey, stepped out with that familiar, warm smile that seemed to light up the sombre façade of Bloodworth Manor.

"Lady Bloodworth," he called, his eyes twinkling with mischief and something deeper. "I do hope I'm not imposing."

Evelyn's carefully cultivated composure wavered. "Archie," she breathed, closing the distance between them in quick, measured steps. Without a word, they embraced, the gesture speaking volumes of their unspoken connection.

Pulling back, Archie's gaze swept over her face. "My word, Evelyn," he murmured. "You're even more radiant than I remembered."

Evelyn felt a blush creep up her neck. "And you, sir, are as silver-tongued as ever," she retorted, a smile playing on her lips.

"Shall we take a turn about the gardens?" Archie offered his arm. "I'd love to see how your roses are faring."

As they strolled among the blooming flowers, Evelyn found herself relaxing. "I've missed this," she admitted, glancing at Archie. "Your visits always brought such life to the manor."

Archie chuckled, the sound warming her. "And I've missed your sharp wit, my lady. Tell me, has old Julien finally learned to appreciate it?"

Evelyn's smile faltered slightly. "Julien... appreciates what he wishes to," she said carefully. "But let's not speak of him. How have you been, truly?"

"Honestly?" Archie's eyes softened. "I've thought of you often, Evelyn. These past few years have been... lacking, without your presence."

Evelyn's heart skipped a beat. "I... I've thought of you, too," she confessed, her voice barely above a whisper. "More than I should, perhaps."

They paused beneath a flowering arbour, the sweet scent of roses enveloping them. Archie turned to face her, his expression serious. "Evelyn, I—"

But whatever he was about to say was

interrupted by a distant call from the house. Evelyn stepped back, reality crashing back in. "We should return," she said, reluctance clear in her voice. "The others will be waiting."

As they walked back, Evelyn's mind raced. What had Archie been about to say? And more importantly, what would she have done if he'd said it?

The golden light of the setting sun danced across the lake's surface, casting a warm glow over Evelyn and Archie as they sat on a blanket near the water's edge. A wicker basket lay open between them, filled with an assortment of delicate pastries and fresh fruits.

Evelyn reached for a strawberry, her fingers accidentally brushing against Archie's as he did the same. A jolt of electricity seemed to pass between them, and she quickly withdrew her hand, her cheeks flushing.

"My apologies," Archie said with a gentle smile, offering her the fruit. "Ladies first, of course."

Evelyn accepted it with a shy nod. "Thank you, Archie. It's... it's been so long since I've done something like this."

"A picnic by the lake?" Archie asked, his tone light but his eyes searching.

She sighed, her gaze drifting to the shimmering water. "Anything that brings me joy, really," she admitted softly.

Archie's brow furrowed with concern. "Evelyn, is everything alright? You seem... different from when I last saw you."

Evelyn felt a lump form in her throat. How could she possibly explain her life in this manor? In this life that had felt like anything but her own since the very moment she'd crossed the threshold those seven years previous? She had tried so hard to maintain a façade of contentment, but Archie's genuine concern broke through her defences.

"I..." she began, her voice trembling. "Life with Julien is... challenging. When he's here, I feel as though I'm suffocating. The air itself seems heavier, colder." She wrapped her arms around herself, as if warding off a chill. "And when he's gone on business, like now, I... I find myself wishing he'd never return."

Archie listened intently, his eyes never leaving her face. Gently, he reached out and placed his hand over hers. "I had no idea it was so difficult for you," he said softly. "Is there anything I can do?"

Evelyn felt tears prickling at the corners of her eyes. "Your presence alone is a comfort, Archie. When you're here, I can breathe again. I feel... seen. Understood."

"You are seen, Evelyn," Archie said, his voice filled with warmth and determination. "And you deserve so much more than this life of fear and oppression."

She looked up at him, her green eyes shining with unshed tears. "But what can I do? Julien holds all the power. I have nowhere to go, and I can't leave—"

"Your son," Archie finished her thought for her, understanding dawning in his eyes. "Of course. Your maternal instincts are one of the things I admire most about you, Evelyn."

His words wrapped around her like a warm embrace, offering strength and solace. For a moment, Evelyn allowed herself to imagine a different life, one where she could be truly happy. But the reality of her situation quickly reasserted itself.

"Thank you for listening, Archie," she said, squeezing his hand. "Your understanding means more to me than you know."

As the sun dipped lower on the horizon, casting long shadows across the lake, Evelyn felt a bittersweet mix of comfort and longing. Archie's presence was a balm to her weary soul, but it also served as a stark reminder of everything she could never have.

The crackling fire in the drawing room cast dancing shadows across the ornate wallpaper, mirroring the tumultuous emotions within Evelyn's heart. She sat close to Archie on the plush settee, their thighs nearly touching. The heat from his body seemed to radiate through her, igniting a warmth that had nothing to do with the nearby flames.

Evelyn's eyes flickered to Archie's face, tracing the strong line of his jaw, the curve of his lips. Her breath caught in her throat as she realised, he was watching her, too, his gaze intense and filled with an emotion she dared not name.

"Evelyn," Archie murmured, his voice low and husky. "I..."

Words failed him, and in that charged silence, Evelyn felt the world narrow to just the two of them. Her heart raced, anticipation thrumming through her veins.

Slowly, deliberately, Archie leaned in. Evelyn's eyes fluttered closed as his lips met hers, soft and warm. The kiss was gentle at first, a question, an offering. Then, as if a dam had broken, it deepened with a sudden, fierce passion that left her breathless.

When they finally parted, Evelyn's cheeks were flushed, her lips tingling. "Archie," she whispered, her voice trembling. "We shouldn't..."

"I know," he replied, resting his forehead against hers. "But I can't deny my feelings for you any longer, Evelyn. You've captured my heart entirely."

The days that followed were a whirlwind of stolen moments and secret meetings. Evelyn felt as though she were living in a dream, one from which she never wanted to wake. They would sneak away to the rose garden, hidden from prying eyes by lush greenery, to share passionate kisses and tender embraces.

"You're positively glowing, my dear," Archie remarked one afternoon as they strolled arm-in-arm through a secluded part of the estate.

Evelyn laughed, a sound of pure joy that she hadn't realised she was still capable of making. "I feel... free," she admitted. "When I'm with you, I can forget about everything else. It's as if the world outside doesn't exist."

But even as she revelled in her newfound happiness, a nagging fear lurked at the edges of her consciousness. Julien's imminent return loomed over her like a storm cloud, threatening to shatter this fragile paradise she and Archie had created.

"What are we going to do?" Evelyn asked one evening, her voice barely above a whisper as they sat hidden in the library alcove.

Archie's arms tightened around her. "We'll find a way," he promised. "I won't let him hurt you again, Evelyn. I swear it."

She wanted to believe him, to trust in the strength of their love. But as she nestled closer to Archie, inhaling his comforting scent, Evelyn couldn't quite shake the dread that coiled in her stomach. The clock was ticking, and soon their stolen summer would come to an end.

The warm afternoon sun filtered through the leaves of the old oak tree, casting dappled shadows on Evelyn and Archie as they sat side by side on a weathered stone bench in the garden. Evelyn's emerald eyes shimmered with a mix of hope and trepidation as she turned to face Archie.

"What do you see for us, Archie?" she asked, her voice soft but tinged with longing. "Beyond these walls, beyond... all of this?"

Archie's tousled fair hair caught the sunlight as he smiled, his eyes twinkling with that familiar mischief. "I see a little cottage by the sea," he began, taking her hand in his. "You, me, and young Edgar, free to live as we please. No more shadows, no more fear."

Evelyn's heart fluttered at the image, but she couldn't help the pang of anxiety that followed. "It sounds like a dream," she murmured, her gaze dropping to their intertwined fingers. "But Julien... he would never allow it. And what of my duties here?"

Archie gently lifted her chin, his expression earnest. "You've carried those duties long enough, Evelyn. You deserve happiness, true happiness."

She closed her eyes, leaning into his touch. "I'm not as afraid of him as I once was," she admitted. "But the consequences if we were discovered..."

"We'll be careful," Archie assured her, his voice low and determined. "We can plan, prepare. There's always a way, if we're brave enough to take it."

As Evelyn opened her mouth to respond, a cool breeze rustled through the garden, carrying with it the faint sound of approaching footsteps. They quickly separated; their moment of intimacy shattered.

"My lady," called the housekeeper's voice, growing nearer. "A message has arrived for you."

Evelyn's stomach clenched as she rose to meet the older woman. The letter she was handed bore Julien's unmistakable seal. With trembling fingers, she broke it open, her eyes scanning the contents.

"He's coming back," she whispered, her face paling. "Within the fortnight."

Archie stood, moving closer but not daring to touch her with the housekeeper present. "How long?" he asked, his voice taut with concern.

"Two weeks, at most," Evelyn replied, her mind racing. She turned to the housekeeper, composing herself. "Thank you, Maggie. Please begin preparations for the Marquis's return."

As the woman hurried away, Evelyn's carefully constructed façade crumbled. She looked at Archie, her eyes wide with fear.

"Our time is running out," she breathed, the

weight of their predicament crushing down upon her.

The sun had long since set, casting Evelyn's bedchamber in a warm, intimate glow from the flickering candles. Archie stood by the window; his silhouette etched against the moonlit sky. He turned to face Evelyn, his eyes brimming with an intensity she had never seen before.

"Evelyn," he began, his voice barely above a whisper, "I can't bear the thought of losing you again." He crossed the room in quick strides, taking her hands in his. "I love you. I've loved you for so long, and I can't keep it inside any longer."

Evelyn's breath caught in her throat. "Archie, I—"

But his lips were on hers before she could finish, passionate and urgent. She melted into his embrace, her body responding with a fervour she had never known. Their kisses deepened, hands exploring, clothes falling away until they tumbled onto the bed in a tangle of limbs.

Their lovemaking was tender yet passionate, nothing like the cold, dutiful encounters she had endured with Julien. Archie's touch ignited a fire within her, each caress and kiss burning away the years of loneliness and fear.

Afterward, as they lay entwined, Archie propped himself up on one elbow, his eyes searching hers. "Run away with me, Evelyn," he pleaded. "We can start a new life together, far from here. You deserve happiness and freedom."

Evelyn's heart soared at his words, but a familiar dread crept in. She sat up, pulling the sheet around her. "But Edgar... Julien would never let us go. He'd hunt us down, and the consequences..."

Archie cupped her face gently. "We'll find a way to protect Edgar. I promise you; I'll do everything in my power to keep you both safe."

Evelyn bit her lower lip, her mind a whirlwind of conflicting emotions. "I want to say yes," she whispered, tears welling in her eyes. "God, how I want to. But the risk..."

"Is it not worth taking for a chance at true happiness?" Archie asked, his voice filled with hope and determination.

Evelyn closed her eyes, her heart and mind waging a furious battle. The promise of freedom and love beckoned, but the image of Edgar, alone and at Julien's mercy, haunted her. She opened her eyes, meeting Archie's expectant gaze.

"I need time," she said softly. "To think, to plan. We can't rush into this blindly."

Archie nodded, understanding in his eyes. "Of course. We have two weeks before Julien returns. We'll use that time wisely."

As Evelyn lay back down, nestling into Archie's embrace, she felt both exhilarated and terrified. The possibility of a new life tantalised her, but the spectre of Julien's wrath loomed large. She knew that whatever decision she made would alter the course of her life forever.

The moonlight filtered through the gauzy curtains, casting a soft glow on Evelyn and Archie as they lay entwined in each other's arms. The ticking of the mantle clock seemed to echo their dwindling moments together, each second a painful reminder of their impending separation.

Evelyn traced her fingers along Archie's jawline, memorising every contour. "I wish we could freeze time," she whispered, her voice thick with emotion.

Archie pulled her closer, pressing a tender kiss to her forehead. "We still have tonight, my love. Let's make it count."

"Tell me again," Evelyn implored, her emerald eyes searching his. "Tell me about the life we could have."

Archie's eyes sparkled with warmth as he spoke. "We'll find a quiet cottage by the sea. You'll have a garden filled with roses, and I'll read poetry to you as the sun sets. We'll be free, Evelyn. Free to love, to laugh, to live."

Tears welled in Evelyn's eyes. "It sounds like a beautiful dream."

"It doesn't have to be just a dream," Archie insisted, his voice gentle but fervent. "Say the word, and I'll make it our reality."

Evelyn's heart constricted. "Oh, Archie. If only it were that simple." She paused, her thoughts turning to Edgar. "I can't bear the thought of leaving him behind."

Archie wiped away a tear that had escaped down her cheek. "You'll never have to. We'll find a way, I swear it. Whatever it takes, we'll bring Edgar with us."

As the night deepened, they whispered promises and shared tender caresses, each touch bittersweet with the knowledge of their looming goodbye. When dawn finally broke, Evelyn felt as though her heart was being torn in two.

Standing at the grand entrance of Bloodworth Manor, Evelyn watched as the footmen loaded Archie's luggage into the waiting carriage. The morning mist clung to the grounds, shrouding the world in a dreamlike haze.

Archie approached her, his eyes filled with a mixture of love and sorrow. "This isn't goodbye," he said softly, taking her hands in his. "It's just until we meet again."

Evelyn nodded, unable to speak past the lump in her throat. She longed to throw caution to the wind, to climb into the carriage beside him and never look back. But the thought of Edgar, her beautiful little boy still sleeping peacefully in his nursery, held her in place.

As Archie's carriage rolled down the long drive, Evelyn's mind flashed back to that day three years ago when he had left before. The ache in her chest was familiar, yet infinitely more intense now that she knew the depth of their love.

She remained rooted to the spot long after the carriage had disappeared from view, her heart heavy with the weight of what could have been. The future loomed before her, filled with uncertainty and the daunting prospect of facing Julien's return.

Slowly, Evelyn turned back towards the manor, its imposing façade a stark reminder of the gilded cage that held her. With each step, she steeled herself for the challenges ahead, clinging to the hope that someday, somehow, she and Archie would find their way back to each other.

Chapter 10

The Fruits of Passion

The faded ink on the small, worn calendar seemed to mock Evelyn as her trembling fingers traced the dates. Her emerald eyes widened, heart thundering against her ribs as the realisation struck her like a bolt of lightning. She was late.

"No," she whispered, her voice barely audible in the oppressive silence of her chambers. "It can't be."

But the evidence was there, stark and undeniable on the yellowed page before her. Evelyn's mind reeled, memories of passionate stolen moments with Archie flooding back in a dizzying rush. His tousled fair hair, those mischievous eyes, the warmth of his embrace...

She pushed away from the writing desk; her legs unsteady as she began to pace the room. The opulent surroundings of Bloodworth Manor felt suddenly suffocating, closing in around her like a gilded cage.

"What have I done?" Evelyn murmured; one hand pressed against her still-flat abdomen. "A child... Archie's child."

The magnitude of her situation crashed over her in waves. This was no mere indiscretion, no fleeting affair that could be swept under the rug. This was a life, growing within her—a life that would shatter the carefully maintained façade of her marriage to Julien.

Evelyn's thoughts raced, her internal monologue a frantic jumble of fear and desperate planning. *Julien can never know. He'd... he'd destroy us both. But how can I hide this? How long before it becomes obvious?*

She paused by the window, staring out at the manicured gardens below without truly seeing them. Her reflection in the glass seemed a stranger—pale, wide-eyed, on the precipice of a life-altering decision.

"I have to leave," Evelyn realised, the words escaping her lips in a shaky exhale. "For the sake of this child... for my own sake. I can't stay here, not for this."

With newfound determination, she squared her shoulders, her innate strength rising to meet the monumental challenge before her. *I'll find a way*, Evelyn vowed to her reflection, to the innocent life nestled within her.

"Oh, Archie," Evelyn sighed, her voice a mixture of longing and resolve. "What will you say when you learn of this? Will you stand by us, or will the weight of your family's expectations prove too much?"

She resumed her pacing, each step bringing fresh waves of anxiety and determination. The future stretched before her; a winding path shrouded in uncertainty.

"Whatever comes," she whispered fiercely, one hand protectively cradling her own body, "I'll face it. For you."

Evelyn's eyes flickered towards the door, her heart racing as she contemplated her next move. The weight of her secret pressed upon her, urging her to action. With trembling fingers, she smoothed her auburn hair and straightened her posture, drawing on the quiet strength that had sustained her through years of isolation in Bloodworth Manor.

"Florence," she whispered, the name a talisman of hope. "I must speak with Florence."

Her feet carried her swiftly through the labyrinthine corridors, each step echoing with purpose. As she descended the stairs towards the kitchen, Evelyn's resolve wavered momentarily.

Can I truly burden her with this? she thought, hesitating at the threshold. But the urgency of her situation, the life growing within her, propelled her forward.

The kitchen's warmth enveloped Evelyn as she entered, a stark contrast to the cold dread in her heart. Florence stood by the hearth; her kind face illuminated by the dancing flames. For a moment, Evelyn simply watched her, drinking in the comforting presence of her most trusted ally within the house.

"Florence," Evelyn called softly, her voice barely above a whisper. "Might I have a word?"

Florence turned, her eyes brightening at the sight of Evelyn. "Of course, my lady. Is everything alright?"

Evelyn glanced around, ensuring their privacy. "Not here," she murmured, gently taking Florence's arm. "Somewhere more... discreet."

As they moved to a quiet corner, Evelyn's thoughts raced. *How do I begin? Will she understand? Will she judge me?* But as she met Florence's concerned gaze, she found the courage to speak.

"Florence, I... I find myself in a delicate situation," Evelyn began, her voice trembling slightly. "One that requires absolute discretion and... and your help."

Florence's brow furrowed with concern. "My lady, you know you can trust me with anything. What troubles you so?"

Evelyn took a deep breath, steeling herself. "I'm pregnant, Florence," she whispered, her words barely audible. "And the father... the father is not Lord Bloodworth."

Florence's eyes widened, a mix of surprise and concern flashing across her face. For a moment, Evelyn's heart clenched, fearing judgment or rejection. But then Florence's expression softened, her warm hands clasping Evelyn's trembling ones.

"Oh, my dear," Florence breathed, her voice filled with compassion. "You must be so frightened. But fear not, we'll find a way through this together."

Relief washed over Evelyn, her eyes brimming with tears. "You'll help me?" she whispered, hope flickering in her chest.

Florence nodded firmly. "Of course, my lady. Your secret is safe with me. Now, we must devise a plan to protect you and the little one."

Evelyn's mind raced. "But how? I can't stay here. If Julien discovers..."

"Hush now," Florence soothed, glancing around to ensure they weren't overheard. "What we need is a reason for you to leave the manor, one that won't arouse suspicion."

Evelyn bit her lip, considering. "But what could possibly—"

"An illness," Florence interjected, her eyes brightening with inspiration. "Given the stress you've been under, it would be entirely believable for you to fall ill and require a change of air."

"An illness," Evelyn repeated, turning the idea over in her mind. It seemed plausible, yet fear still gnawed at her. "But Julien—"

"Will be all too eager to have you recuperate elsewhere, away from his precious routines," Florence finished, a hint of bitterness in her tone. "We'll make it convincing, my lady. A few days of feigned weakness, some well-placed comments about the benefits of country air..."

As Florence outlined the plan, Evelyn felt a glimmer of hope. "It could work," she murmured, her hand unconsciously moving to her still-flat stomach. "But where would I go?"

Florence leaned in closer, her voice dropping to a whisper. "My sister has a small cottage near the coast. It's secluded, quiet—perfect for a lady in need of rest." Her eyes sparkled with determination. "I'll send word ahead, prepare everything for your arrival."

Evelyn nodded, her mind whirling with details. "How long should I wait before I fall ill?"

"Three days," Florence replied decisively. "We'll start with fatigue, then progress to dizzy spells. By the fourth day, you'll be too weak to leave your bed."

"And the journey?" Evelyn asked, her eyes clouding with worry.

Florence patted her hand reassuringly. "Leave that to me, my lady. I'll arrange for a trusted driver and a comfortable carriage. You'll need to pack lightly—just essentials. My sister's household has a small number of staff who would be more than happy to accommodate you while you're there."

Evelyn's heart raced, hope and fear battling within her. "Florence, I—I don't know how to thank you."

"There's no need," Florence smiled warmly. "Now, you should return to your chambers. We can't arouse suspicion."

Later that evening, Evelyn stood before her wardrobe, a small trunk open on her bed. Her hands trembled slightly as she reached for a simple gown.

"What does one pack," she murmured to herself, "when fleeing one's life?"

She folded the gown carefully, laying it in the trunk. As she turned back to select another, her eyes caught her reflection in the mirror. The woman staring back seemed both familiar and strange—her features the same, but her eyes holding a new resolve.

"You can do this," Evelyn whispered to her reflection. "For the child. For yourself." For Edgar."

Her fingers brushed against a soft shawl, a gift from her mother years ago, when she'd first left home at seventeen to come to Bloodworth Manor. She clutched it to her chest, inhaling its faint lavender scent. "Oh, Mother," she sighed. "What would you say if you could see me now?"

Shaking off the moment of melancholy, Evelyn returned to her task. Each item she placed in the trunk felt like a step towards an uncertain future. A future that, despite its dangers, held the only hope she had.

As she folded a final nightgown, Evelyn's hand instinctively moved to her stomach. "We'll be alright, little one," she whispered. "I promise."

Evelyn's gaze drifted to her writing desk, the pristine parchment awaiting her words. With a deep breath, she settled into the chair, her fingers wrapping around the delicate quill. The weight of what she was about to do pressed upon her like a physical force.

"How does one convey such urgency without revealing too much?" she murmured, her green eyes narrowing in concentration.

She began to write, her hand moving with practiced grace:

My dearest friend,

The roses bloom early this year, their petals unfurling with unexpected haste. I find myself in need of your gardening expertise, as the thorns have grown sharp and treacherous...

Evelyn paused, biting her lip. "Will he understand?" she wondered aloud, her voice barely above a whisper.

As if in response, a gentle knock sounded at the door. Florence's warm voice called out, "My lady? Is everything alright?"

"Yes, Florence. Please, come in," Evelyn replied, hastily covering the letter with a blank sheet.

Florence entered, her kind eyes immediately finding Evelyn's. "I thought you might need some assistance," she said softly.

Evelyn's shoulders relaxed slightly at her friend's presence. "Florence, I... I'm writing to Archie. But how can I tell him without truly telling him?"

Florence approached, laying a comforting hand on Evelyn's shoulder. "Your bond with Mr. Bates is strong, my lady. Trust in that. He'll understand your need, even if he doesn't know the specifics. That can wait."

Nodding, Evelyn returned to her task, carefully crafting each sentence to convey her desperation without explicit details. As she wrote, she could feel her heart racing, hope and fear warring within her chest.

The morning sun cast long shadows across Bloodworth Manor, its golden rays unable to penetrate the palpable tension that hung in the air. Evelyn lay in her bed, her face ashen and drawn, playing the part of an ailing lady with convincing authenticity.

A soft knock preceded Florence's entrance. "My lady," she said, her voice low and concerned, "how are you feeling this morning?"

Evelyn turned her head weakly, her eyes meeting Florence's. "I fear I'm not improving, Florence," she murmured, her voice rough with feigned illness. "Perhaps... perhaps it's time to consider that journey for my health we discussed."

Florence nodded, understanding passing between them. "Of course, my lady. I'll make the arrangements at once."

As Florence bustled about the room, gathering Evelyn's things, Evelyn allowed her thoughts to wander. *Will this work?* she wondered, her hand unconsciously moving to rest on her lower abdomen. *Can I truly escape?*

Hours passed in a flurry of hushed preparations and whispered conversations. Finally, as the afternoon sun began its descent, Evelyn found herself standing before the manor's grand entrance, a small trunk at her feet.

Florence appeared at her side, pressing a warm shawl into Evelyn's hands. "For the journey, my lady," she said, her eyes shining with unshed tears.

Evelyn clasped Florence's hands, her grip tight with emotion. "I don't know how to thank you," she whispered, her voice thick.

"There's no need," Florence replied, squeezing Evelyn's hands. "Your safety, your happiness—that's all the thanks I require."

They stood for a moment, volumes passing

between them in silence. Then, with a deep breath, Evelyn straightened her shoulders. "I'm ready," she said, her voice steady despite the tumult in her heart.

As she stepped towards the waiting carriage, Florence's voice called out softly, "Be safe, my lady. And remember, you're stronger than you know."

Evelyn paused, turning back to offer a small, grateful smile. Then, gathering her courage, she climbed into the carriage, the door closing behind her with a soft thud of finality.

The carriage lurched forward, wheels crunching against gravel as Bloodworth Manor began to recede. Evelyn's eyes fixed on the imposing structure, a maelstrom of emotions churning within her.

"Freedom," she whispered, her breath fogging the glass. Yet even as relief flooded her veins, anxiety coiled in her stomach. "What have I done?"

The landscape blurred past, a tapestry of autumn colours mirroring her tumultuous thoughts. Fields of gold gave way to dense forests, their branches reaching out like grasping fingers.

"I had to leave," Evelyn murmured, her hand instinctively moving to her abdomen. "For you, little one. For your brother. For us all."

She closed her eyes, remembering Edgar's face as she'd bid him farewell. The pain of separation from her son clawed at her heart, but she pushed it aside. *He's still young, he won't remember a few months...* she told herself, though doubt lingered.

As the carriage rounded a bend, Evelyn caught a final glimpse of Bloodworth Manor. The sight of it, growing smaller in the distance, sparked a fierce determination within her.

"No more fear," she declared, her voice growing stronger. "No more living under his shadow." Her fingers curled into fists, nails biting into her palms. "I will protect this child, come what may."

The manor had long disappeared from view, and with it, the last vestiges of Evelyn's hesitation. She sat straighter, her chin lifted in defiance of the challenges ahead.

"We're going to be alright," she whispered to her unborn child, a small smile tugging at her lips. "I promise you that."

Chapter 11

A Mother's Sacrifice

Evelyn gripped the edge of the wooden bed, her knuckles white with strain. Another contraction tore through her body, and she bit back a cry, her emerald eyes flashing with determination. The modest room of the coastal cottage, so different from the opulent chambers of Bloodworth Manor, seemed to close in around her.

"Breathe, Evelyn," she reminded herself, her voice barely a whisper. "For the child. For yourself."

As the pain subsided momentarily, Evelyn's thoughts raced. How had she come to this? From a sheltered girl thrust into an arranged marriage, to a woman now giving birth in secret, far from the watchful eyes of her husband. The irony wasn't lost on her.

A gentle knock interrupted her reverie, and the door creaked open. A woman with kind eyes and greying hair stepped in, her movements fluid and assured.

"Good evening, Mrs. Appleby," the midwife said, her voice soothing. "Let's see how you're faring, shall we?"

Evelyn nodded, grateful for the woman's calm demeanour, thankful she'd used her maiden name, so as not to attract attention to her predicament. "Thank you for coming," she managed, her words clipped as another contraction began to build.

The midwife moved with practiced ease, checking Evelyn's progress and offering words of encouragement. "You're doing wonderfully, dear. The babe will be here soon."

As the pain intensified, Evelyn found herself clinging to the midwife's steadying presence. It was a stark contrast to the cold, clinical atmosphere she'd come from those few months previous.

"I... I've never done this before," Evelyn lied between laboured breaths, a hint of vulnerability creeping into her usually composed tone. She couldn't let anyone outside the household know where she'd come from, who she really was... who she really belonged to.

The midwife patted her hand. "Few have on their first go. But you've got the strength in you, I can see it plain as day."

Evelyn managed a weak smile, drawing on

reserves of determination she didn't know she possessed, yet knowing perfectly well that it was become she'd done this once before. As another contraction gripped her, she focused on her breathing, on the future she was fighting for.

"That's it, love," the midwife encouraged. "Let your body do what it knows how to do."

In that moment, surrounded by the simple furnishings of the cottage and guided by the midwife's gentle expertise, Evelyn felt a peculiar sense of freedom. Here, she wasn't Lady Bloodworth, bound by the expectations of her title. She was simply Evelyn, a woman bringing new life into the world.

"Tell me," Evelyn gasped between contractions, "have you delivered many babies?"

The midwife chuckled softly. "More than I can count, my dear. Each one a miracle in its own right."

As the pain intensified, Evelyn closed her eyes, picturing the child she was about to meet. A child born of love, if not of a sanctioned union. A child who would need protection from the very first breath.

"You're almost there," the midwife's voice cut through her thoughts. "One more big push ought to do it."

Evelyn steeled herself, drawing on every ounce

of strength she possessed. In this moment, she wasn't just fighting for herself, but for the future of her child. With a determination that surprised even her, she pushed, her emerald eyes flashing with an indomitable will.

A piercing cry filled the air, and suddenly, the world shifted. Evelyn felt a surge of relief wash over her, mingled with an overwhelming joy that brought tears to her eyes. Her breath caught in her throat as she heard her baby's first cries, a sound more beautiful than any symphony.

"Oh, my darling," Evelyn whispered, her voice trembling with emotion. "You're here at last."

The midwife placed the tiny, squirming bundle in Evelyn's arms, and in that instant, a profound connection blossomed. Evelyn gazed down at her daughter, marvelling at the miracle she held.

"A girl. She's perfect," the midwife said softly. "You've done wonderfully, love."

Evelyn barely heard her, lost in the wonder of her child. With trembling fingers, she traced the delicate features of her daughter's face—the tiny nose, the rosebud lips, the impossibly soft cheeks.

"Hello, my sweet," Evelyn murmured, her voice thick with emotion. "I've waited so long to meet you."

As she studied her daughter's face, Evelyn felt a whirlwind of emotions. Love, fierce and protective, surged through her. Hope for the future bloomed in her heart. Yet, lurking beneath it all was the shadow of impending separation.

"She has your eyes," the midwife observed. "They'll likely darken with time, but for now, they're as bright green as yours."

Evelyn nodded, unable to speak past the lump in her throat. She pressed a gentle kiss to her daughter's forehead, inhaling the sweet scent of new life.

"I wish..." Evelyn began, then faltered. How could she express the depth of her longing, her fear, her determination? "I wish things could be different," she said finally, her voice barely above a whisper.

Evelyn took a deep breath, her bright eyes shimmering with unshed tears. "Elspeth," she whispered, her voice filled with reverence and love. "Your name shall be Elspeth. And I'll make sure your daddy knows to keep it for you."

The midwife tilted her head, a gentle smile gracing her weathered features. "A beautiful name, my dear. Does it hold special meaning?"

Evelyn nodded, her gaze never leaving her daughter's face. "It means 'chosen by God,'" she explained, her voice soft but resolute. "For she is truly a blessing, a symbol of hope for the future I dream of."

As she spoke, Evelyn's fingers gently caressed

Elspeth's cheek, her touch as light as a butterfly's wing. In her mind, she saw flashes of the life she wished for her daughter—one filled with love, laughter, and freedom; one so very different from her own. If she could wish anything for her daughter, it was that.

The midwife cleared her throat softly, breaking the spell of the moment. "My dear," she began, her tone gentle but firm, "I hate to disturb you, but we must discuss the arrangements for the child's journey to London, as I believe it to be."

Evelyn's heart clenched, but she forced herself to meet the midwife's kind eyes. "Yes, of course," she replied, her voice steady despite the turmoil within. "Tell me, how soon can she safely travel?"

The midwife moved closer, her presence reassuring. "I've made all the necessary preparations. I give you my word that young Elspeth will be safe and comfortable on her journey to Mr. Bates."

Evelyn's thoughts turned to Archie, his warm smile and kind eyes a balm to her worried heart. "And you're certain Archie will be there to receive her?" she asked, unable to keep the note of anxiety from her voice.

The kind midwife nodded, her expression calm and confident. "I've received confirmation from Mr. Bates himself. He awaits the child's arrival with great anticipation and has assured me of his plans for her to be cared for."

Evelyn closed her eyes briefly, drawing strength from the knowledge that her beloved Archie would protect their daughter. When she opened them again, there was a quiet determination in her gaze. "Very well," she said softly. "Let us prepare for Elspeth's journey."

Evelyn's eyes glistened as she gazed down at Elspeth, her heart swelling with a fierce, protective love. She traced the delicate curve of her daughter's cheek, memorising every detail of her perfect face. The weight of the impending separation pressed heavily upon her, threatening to shatter her resolve.

"My darling," Evelyn whispered, her voice trembling, "how can I bear to let you go?"

The midwife placed a gentle hand on Evelyn's shoulder. "It's time, my dear. We must not delay if we're to ensure her safe passage."

Evelyn nodded, swallowing hard. "I know. It's just..." She paused, struggling to find the words. "She's so small, so vulnerable. What if she needs me?"

"She'll be well cared for, I assure you," the midwife said softly. "And Mr. Bates will ensure she is loved."

With a deep, shuddering breath, Evelyn lifted Elspeth into her arms one last time. She pressed a tender kiss to her daughter's forehead, inhaling her sweet scent.

"Be brave, my little one," she murmured, her words a solemn vow. "One day, I swear to you, we'll be together again."

Tears blurring her vision, Evelyn carefully placed Elspeth into the midwife's waiting arms. Her hands lingered, reluctant to break contact with her precious child.

As the midwife cradled Elspeth, Evelyn's thoughts raced. How would she find her way back to her daughter? When would it be safe? The uncertainty of it all threatened to overwhelm her, but she forced herself to stand tall, channelling the quiet strength that had become her armour.

"Take care of her," Evelyn said, her voice low and intense. "Promise me you'll protect her with your life."

The midwife met her gaze steadily. "You have my word. I'll guard her as if she were my own flesh and blood."

The door closed with a soft click, and suddenly, the room was engulfed in silence. Evelyn sat motionless, her arms aching with the phantom weight of her child. The absence of Elspeth's cries left a void so profound it seemed to echo off the bare walls.

Evelyn's eyes darted to the empty cradle, then to

the rumpled sheets where she had laboured. "How quickly it all changes," she whispered to herself, her voice barely audible. The joy of birth and the sorrow of parting intertwined, leaving her heart in a tumultuous state.

She stood gently from her bed place and moved to the window, pressing her forehead against the cool glass. "I must be strong," Evelyn murmured, her breath fogging the pane. "For Elspeth. For Edgar." The thought of her son waiting at Bloodworth Manor bolstered her resolve.

Taking a deep breath, Evelyn smoothed her dress and turned to face her reflection in a small mirror. Her features, though weary, held a quiet dignity. "You are Lady Bloodworth," she reminded herself firmly. "You've endured worse than this."

The next day, as she gathered her belongings, a small cry escaped her lips. "Oh, Elspeth," she breathed, closing her eyes briefly. "Will you forgive me when you're older? Will you understand why I had to do this?"

Evelyn shook her head, forcing the doubts away. She squared her shoulders, lifted her chin, and strode towards the door. The grace with which she carried herself belied the weight of her secret.

"Back to Bloodworth Manor," she said aloud, her tone resolute. "Back to the lion's den." A wry smile curved her lips as she thought of Julien's icy demeanour. "But this lioness has claws of her own now."

With one last glance at the room where her daughter had been born, Evelyn stepped out, ready to face whatever challenges lay ahead. The door closed behind her with a soft thud, marking the end of one chapter and the beginning of another.

Evelyn stepped out into the crisp morning air, her green eyes squinting against the bright sunlight. The coastal village sprawled before her, a patchwork of thatched roofs and winding cobblestone streets. The salty breeze kissed her cheeks, carrying with it the distant rhythm of crashing waves.

For a moment, she allowed herself to breathe deeply, savouring the tang of sea air. "If only..." she murmured, her words carried away by the wind.

A fisherman's wife passed by, nodding respectfully. "Good day, ma'am. I hope you found your stay agreeable?"

Evelyn's lips curved into a polite smile, the mask of Lady Bloodworth slipping effortlessly into place. "Indeed, thank you. Your village is quite charming."

As the woman continued on her way, Evelyn's gaze drifted towards the horizon where sea met sky. The tranquillity of the scene stood in stark contrast to the turmoil in her heart.

Come now, she chided herself softly. *This is no*

time for idle dreams.

With a deep breath, Evelyn took her first step towards the carriage that would carry her back to Bloodworth Manor. Her stride was purposeful, her head held high despite the heaviness in her heart. Each step carried her further from Elspeth, yet closer to the life she must protect.

"One day," she whispered to herself, "one day, my darling Elspeth will know the truth. And on that day, I pray she'll understand why I had to leave her behind."

As she walked, Evelyn's mind raced with plans and contingencies. She had to be prepared for Julien's questions, for the prying eyes of the staff. Her hand unconsciously drifted to her stomach, now flat where it had once been so recently swollen with child.

"For Elspeth," she murmured, her voice barely audible. "For Edgar. For the family we could have been."

With each turn of the carriage wheels, Lady Evelyn Bloodworth's resolve strengthened. The coastal village receded behind her, taking with it the brief moment of peace she had found. Ahead lay Bloodworth Manor, with all its opulence and shadows. Yet Evelyn ventured on, her green eyes fixed on the horizon, carrying within her the fierce hope of a mother's love.

As Evelyn journeyed onward, her thoughts

swirled like a tempest, memories of Elspeth's tiny features intermingling with visions of Edgar's kind eyes. She clutched the locket around her neck, a tangible reminder of the strength she needed to maintain.

"I must be as unyielding as the cliffs," she whispered to herself, her voice barely audible above the crunch of gravel beneath. "As constant as the tides."

The rolling hills gave way to familiar landscapes, each turn bringing her closer to Bloodworth Manor. Evelyn's heart quickened, a mix of anticipation and dread coursing through her veins.

"Back to Edgar," she breathed, a small smile gracing her lips. "My sweet boy."

As the carriage crested the final hill some hours later, Bloodworth Manor loomed before her, its imposing silhouette a stark contrast to the gentle countryside. Evelyn paused, steeling herself for what lay ahead.

"You can do this," she muttered, smoothing her skirts. "For them."

With a deep breath, the carriage approached the gates. The iron bars swung open with a foreboding creak, and Evelyn stepped out, her emerald eyes scanning the courtyard. As she walked up toward the front of the manor, the great door opened, gaping into the world she'd left behind those few months previous.

"Lady Bloodworth," a servant called, rushing to greet her. "It's so wonderful to have you back."

Evelyn smiled, the mask of Lady Bloodworth sliding effortlessly into place. "The sea air did wonders for my health. I felt it was time to return to my duties."

As she spoke, a flurry of movement caught her eye. Edgar appeared at the top of the stairs, his face lighting up at the sight of his mother.

"Mama!" he babbled, crawling down the steps.

Evelyn's façade cracked, genuine joy seeping through as she opened her arms to her son. "Edgar, my darling. How I've missed you."

Evelyn knelt, embracing Edgar tightly, inhaling the familiar scent of her son. As she pulled back, her eyes searched his face, drinking in every detail.

"You've grown," she said softly, her voice tinged with wonder and a hint of sadness.

Edgar beamed, pulling lightly at her dress where he stood, still uneasy on his little legs, yet much more secure than when she'd left him.

As they walked further into the manor, Evelyn's thoughts drifted to Elspeth. Her heart ached with the weight of her secret, but she pushed the pain aside, focusing on the warmth of Edgar's hand in hers.

While Edgar babbled away excitedly, Evelyn's resolve strengthened. She had made sacrifices, yes, but they were not in vain. Someday, she vowed silently, her family would be whole. Until then, she would endure. She would persevere. For her children, she would move mountains if she had to.

The future stretched before her, uncertain but filled with possibility. And in that possibility lay hope—hope for freedom, for reunion, for a life unshackled by the constraints of Bloodworth Manor. With each step farther into the imposing hold of her home, Evelyn's determination grew. Whatever challenges lay ahead, she would face them. For Elspeth. For Edgar. For the promise of a better tomorrow.

Chapter 12

The Passage of Time

Bones set, bruises lighten, and scars fade away; the world moves on, and tragedies are long forgotten.

Seventeen summers had painted the gardens of Bloodworth Manor in countless hues, each season etching its mark upon the sprawling estate. Evelyn stood at the arched window of her chambers; her emerald eyes fixed upon the solitary figure strolling amidst the blooming roses below.

Edgar. Her son. Her heart.

A gentle breeze rustled the silk curtains, carrying with it the sweet scent of lilacs. Evelyn's fingers traced the cool glass, her reflection overlaying the scene before her. Time had been kind to her, the years adding a quiet dignity to her striking features, but it was Edgar who truly captured her gaze.

"How you've grown, my darling," she whispered, watching as he paused to examine a particularly vibrant bloom. His movements were graceful, deliberate—so unlike the impulsive child he had once been, but just as curious. So unlike his father.

Pride swelled within her chest, mingled with a familiar pang of concern. Edgar's gentle nature, his thoughtful demeanour—these were qualities to be cherished, yet they set him apart in a world that often demanded a harsher disposition. Evelyn's hand unconsciously clenched, her protective instincts rising to the surface.

With a determined nod, she turned from the window and made her way through the manor's winding corridors. The weight of her silk gown whispered against the polished floors as she stepped out into the sun-drenched garden.

"Edgar, my dear," she called softly, approaching her son with a warm smile.

He turned, his kind eyes lighting up at the sight of her.

"Mother," he greeted, offering his arm with a gentlemanly flourish that made Evelyn's heart swell.

As they began to stroll along the winding paths, Evelyn sensed a thoughtful tension in Edgar's posture. "What's on your mind, darling?" she inquired, her tone gentle yet probing.

Edgar sighed; his gaze fixed on the distant horizon. "I've been thinking about my future,

Mother. About the expectations placed upon me as a Bloodworth."

Evelyn's grip on his arm tightened imperceptibly. "And what are your thoughts on the matter?"

"I... I wish to make a difference in the world," Edgar confessed, his voice gaining strength. "Not through mere titles or land holdings, but through genuine action. I've been reading about advancements in agriculture, ways to improve the lives of tenants and labourers. I believe we have a responsibility to those who depend upon us."

Evelyn's chest tightened with a mixture of pride and trepidation. "Those are noble aspirations, Edgar," she said carefully, her mind racing to find the right words. "And ones that speak to your compassionate nature."

They paused beside a burbling fountain, its waters catching the afternoon light. Evelyn turned to face her son, taking in the earnest hope shining in his eyes. She chose her next words with deliberate care.

"The path you speak of may not be an easy one," she began, "but I believe it to be a worthy one. You have a unique opportunity to shape not just your own future, but the futures of many others."

Edgar's brow furrowed slightly. "But Father—"

Evelyn raised a hand, silencing him gently. "Your father has his own vision for the estate, it's true.

But you, my darling, have the chance to forge your own path. To take the best of what you've learned and combine it with your own ideals."

She watched as hope and uncertainty warred across Edgar's features. Her heart ached with the desire to shield him from the challenges that lay ahead, even as she recognised the need to let him find his own way.

"Remember, Edgar," she continued, her voice low and fervent, "true strength lies not in domination, but in the ability to lift others up. Your compassion is not a weakness—it is your greatest asset."

Edgar's shoulders straightened, a new resolve settling over him. "Thank you, Mother," he said, his voice thick with emotion. "Your faith in me... it means everything."

Evelyn smiled, reaching up to cup his cheek. In that moment, she saw not just the man he was becoming, but the boy he had been—the child she had vowed to protect at all costs. Whatever storms lay ahead, she would weather them. For Edgar. For the future he deserved.

"Come," she said, linking her arm through his once more. "Tell me more about these agricultural ideas of yours. I believe we have much to discuss."

As they continued their stroll, Evelyn's mind raced with possibilities. The path ahead would not be easy, but with careful planning and unwavering determination, she would ensure that Edgar had the freedom to become the man he was meant to be—not a shadow of his father, but a light all his own.

As Evelyn and Edgar rounded a corner of the immaculately manicured hedge, a servant appeared, his face a mask of practiced neutrality. "My lord, my lady," he intoned, bowing slightly, "The Marquis requests your presence in the east garden."

The warmth drained from the air, replaced by a palpable tension. Evelyn felt Edgar stiffen beside her, his earlier enthusiasm evaporating like morning dew. She squeezed his arm gently, a silent reassurance.

"Very well," Evelyn replied, her voice steady despite the rapid beating of her heart. "We shall join him presently."

As they approached the east garden, Julien's commanding figure came into view. He stood tall, hands clasped behind his back, his very posture radiating authority. The sunlight glinted off his meticulously styled hair, now sporting far more grey than black in the years since they had first met, casting harsh shadows across his angular features.

"Father," Edgar greeted, his voice carefully neutral.

Julien's steely gaze swept over them both. "Edgar," he acknowledged curtly, before turning to Evelyn. "I trust your afternoon stroll was... illuminating?"

Evelyn met his eyes unflinchingly. "Indeed, my lord. Edgar was sharing some fascinating ideas about estate management."

"Is that so?" Julien's tone was sharp, his attention snapping back to Edgar. "And what grand notions has my heir conjured up today?"

Edgar hesitated, his earlier confidence wavering. Evelyn's heart ached, seeing the light in her son's eyes dim under his father's scrutiny.

"I... I was considering ways to improve crop yields on the tenant farms," Edgar began, his voice growing firmer as he continued. "By implementing crop rotation and introducing new fertilisation techniques, we could significantly increase productivity."

Julien's laugh was cold and brittle. "Tenant farms? My boy, a Bloodworth does not concern himself with the minutiae of farming. Our legacy is built on power and influence, not grubbing in the dirt."

Evelyn watched as Edgar's shoulders slumped almost imperceptibly. She longed to intervene, to shield him from Julien's cutting words, but knew that such an action would only invite further scorn.

"The Bloodworth name," Julien continued, his

voice low and intense, "demands respect. It commands obedience. Your duty is to uphold that legacy, not to play at being a common labourer."

Edgar's jaw tightened, a flicker of defiance in his eyes. "But Father, surely our responsibility extends to the welfare of those under our care?"

Julien's expression hardened. "Our responsibility is to maintain our position. The rest will fall into place."

As Evelyn observed the exchange, her mind raced. How could she protect Edgar's gentle spirit without openly defying Julien? The chasm between father and son seemed to widen with each passing moment, and she felt powerless to bridge it.

Later that day, Evelyn found that her fingers trembled as she slid the polished oak panel aside, revealing a hidden compartment in her study's ornate writing desk. With practiced caution, she extracted a letter, its parchment creased from frequent handling in the mere four days since its arrival. Her emerald eyes darted to the door, ensuring her solitude before unfolding the precious missive.

Archie's familiar scrawl brought an immediate warmth to her chest. She sank into her chair, drinking in his words like a parched traveller at an oasis.

"My dearest Evelyn," she read, her lips moving

silently. "I hope this letter finds you well, though I fear the shadows of Bloodworth Manor grow longer with each passing day."

Evelyn's breath caught as she continued. "I bring news of our dear Elspeth. She flourishes in London, a true Cecil in every way but blood. Her adoptive parents dote on her, and she has grown into a young woman of remarkable grace and kindness."

A bittersweet smile played across Evelyn's lips. She closed her eyes, imagining the child she had given up, now nearly grown. "Oh, Elspeth," she whispered, her heart aching with longing.

Returning to the letter, she read on. "Elspeth's wit and charm have made her quite popular in society circles. She possesses a natural talent for music and often entertains guests with her piano playing. It reminds me so much of you, my love."

Evelyn's fingers traced the words, her mind awash with memories of stolen moments at the manor's pianoforte, Archie's warm laughter echoing in her ears.

"How I wish," Archie's letter continued, "that circumstances were different. That we could all be together, free from the constraints that bind us. But know this, Evelyn: Elspeth is loved, she is safe, and she carries within her the best parts of both of us."

A single tear slid down Evelyn's cheek. "Thank

you, Archie," she murmured, pressing the letter to her heart. "Thank you for giving her the life I couldn't."

With a deep breath, she carefully refolded the letter, her resolve strengthening. She may not have been able to openly mother Elspeth, but she could still protect Edgar from the fate that had nearly destroyed her. As she returned the letter to its hiding place, Evelyn's eyes hardened with determination. She would find a way to secure her son's future, no matter the cost.

The crystal chandelier cast a cold, unforgiving light over the dining room, its prisms refracting shadows across the faces of the Bloodworth family. Evelyn sat rigidly in her high-backed chair; her fingers curled tightly around her silver fork as she pushed a morsel of roast pheasant around her plate. The air hung heavy with unspoken tension, punctuated only by the occasional clink of cutlery against fine china.

Edgar, seated to her right, caught her eye briefly. His kind expression was marred by a furrow between his brows, a silent question passing between them. Evelyn offered him a small, reassuring smile, though her heart ached at the weight she saw on his young shoulders.

At the head of the table, Julien cleared his throat, the sound sharp as a whip crack in the oppressive silence. "Edgar," he began, his steely gaze fixed on his son, "you've come of age now. It's time we discussed your future."

Evelyn's breath caught in her throat; was that not what they had been attempting to do earlier? She set down her fork, her eyes darting between her husband and her son.

"What do you mean, Father?" Edgar asked, his voice steady despite the tension evident in the set of his shoulders.

Julien dabbed at his mouth with a crisp linen napkin before answering. "I've been in correspondence with some of our dear friends in London. They have a daughter, one who would make a suitable match. I intend to begin marriage negotiations immediately."

The words fell like lead in Evelyn's stomach. She gripped the edge of the table, her knuckles white with the effort of maintaining her composure.

No, she thought desperately, *not Edgar. Not like this.*

Edgar's face had drained of colour, his fork clattering against his plate. "But Father, I... I don't even know this woman you speak of."

"You'll have ample time to become acquainted after the wedding," Julien replied dismissively.

"This union will strengthen our family's position considerably. London flourishes by the day."

Evelyn's mind raced, searching for words that might derail this horrifying plan without incurring Julien's wrath. But before she could speak, Edgar's voice cut through the tension.

"And if I refuse?" he asked, a tremor in his words betraying his fear.

Julien's eyes narrowed dangerously. "You won't."

Evelyn's heart pounded in her chest as she watched her son's defiant stance crumble under Julien's icy glare. The familiar feeling of helplessness threatened to overwhelm her, but she pushed it aside, drawing on the strength she'd cultivated over the years.

Not again, she thought fiercely. *I won't let Edgar suffer the same fate I did.*

"Julien," she began, her voice steady despite her inner turmoil, "perhaps we should discuss this further in private. Edgar is still young, and—"

"The matter is settled, Evelyn," Julien cut her off, his tone brooking no argument. "You'd do well to remember your place."

The dinner concluded in suffocating silence, with Edgar barely touching his food and Evelyn's mind whirling with possibilities. As soon as Julien retired to his study, she caught Edgar's eye and nodded towards the garden.

Once outside, enveloped by the comforting scent of roses, Evelyn pulled her son into a tight embrace. "Oh, my darling," she whispered, her voice thick with emotion.

Edgar's shoulders shook slightly. "Mother, I can't... I won't..."

Evelyn pulled back, cupping his face in her hands. "Listen to me, Edgar. You won't have to. I promise you; I will find a way to prevent this."

"But Father—"

"Your father may think he holds all the power, but he underestimates me," Evelyn said, a determined glint in her eye. "We'll find a way out of this, together. Do you trust me?"

Edgar nodded, a flicker of hope crossing his features. "Always, Mother."

Evelyn smiled, her resolve strengthening. "Good."

Evelyn's footsteps echoed softly on the polished wood as she paced the length of her chambers, her eyes darting from one ornate furnishing to another without truly seeing them. Her mind raced, weaving through a labyrinth of potential strategies and their consequences.

"If I were to appeal to Julien's sense of duty..." she muttered, then shook her head. "No, he'd twist it to suit his own purposes."

She paused by the window, her fingers absently tracing the intricate lace curtains. "Perhaps if I could find a suitable match before Julien does? Someone Edgar actually cares for..."

The thought sparked a glimmer of hope, but it quickly faded as she considered the logistics. "But how to introduce him to eligible young women without arousing suspicion?"

Evelyn resumed her pacing, her skirts swishing with each determined step. "I could threaten to expose some of Julien's less savoury business dealings," she mused, a wry smile tugging at her lips. "But that's a last resort. The fallout would be... considerable."

She couldn't help but wince at the idea of exposing the chamber in his quarters... but that could never be.

She sank into the plush armchair by her writing desk, her posture rigid with tension. "Oh, Archie," she whispered, "what I wouldn't give for your counsel right now."

As if summoned by her thoughts, an idea bloomed. Evelyn leaned forward, pulling a sheet of paper towards her with newfound purpose. Her quill scratched across the parchment, giving life to her swirling thoughts:

> My dearest Archie,
>
> I hope this letter finds you well. I write to you in a matter of great urgency concerning Edgar...

Evelyn's hand moved swiftly, pouring out her fears and hopes onto the page. She detailed Julien's plans, her promise to Edgar, and her determination to break the cycle that had trapped her so many years ago.

> ...your insight has always been invaluable to me, Archie. Any advice or support you can offer in this delicate situation would be most welcome. Time is of the essence, and I fear we must act swiftly to safeguard Edgar's future.

She paused, quill hovering over the paper. After a moment's hesitation, she added:

> Your presence, as always, would be a balm to my troubled spirit. Is there any chance you might pay us a visit in the near future?
>
> With deepest affection,
>
> Evelyn

As she sealed the letter, a mix of determination and hope surged through her. "This isn't over, Julien," she murmured, her voice barely audible. "I won't let you dictate our son's fate, like you did mine."

Evelyn rose from her writing desk, the sealed letter clasped tightly in her hand. She crossed the room with measured steps, her eyes fixed on the world beyond her chamber window. The night had settled over Bloodworth Manor, casting long shadows across the manicured gardens where she and Edgar had stood just hours before.

She pressed her forehead against the cool glass, her breath fogging the pane. "Oh, Edgar," she whispered, her voice barely audible. "I won't fail you. Not this time."

The moonlight caught the glint of unshed tears in her eyes, but Evelyn blinked them away, her jaw set with determination. She straightened her shoulders, the letter still held close to her heart.

"Lady Bloodworth?" A soft knock accompanied the maid's voice. "Shall I take that to the post for you?"

Evelyn turned; her expression composed once more. "Yes, thank you, Florence. And please ensure it's sent with the utmost urgency."

As the door closed behind the housemaid, Evelyn returned her gaze to the night-shrouded grounds. Her mind raced with possibilities; each thought a step on the path to Edgar's freedom.

"I was too young, too naïve to fight for myself," she mused, her fingers tracing abstract patterns on the glass. "But for Edgar? For my son? I will move heaven and earth, if I must."

A cool breeze rustled the curtains, and Evelyn inhaled deeply, drawing strength from the crisp night air. Her reflection stared back at her, no longer the timid girl who had first arrived at Bloodworth Manor, but a woman tempered by years of silent resilience.

"Whatever comes," she vowed to the night, her voice low but unwavering, "I'll face it. For Edgar's sake, for the future he deserves. This ends with us."

With one last look at the moonlit gardens, Evelyn turned from the window, her steps purposeful as she moved across the room. The challenges ahead loomed large, but for the first time in years, Lady Evelyn Bloodworth felt truly, irrevocably ready to meet them head-on.

Chapter 13

A Fateful Reunion

The grand hall of Bloodworth Manor fell silent as Julien's commanding voice echoed off the ornate walls. "Edgar, may I present Miss Elspeth Cecil."

Evelyn's heart lurched in her chest as she heard the name, her fingers tightening around the delicate stem of her champagne flute. Time seemed to slow as she watched her son step forward, his polite smile faltering for just a moment as he took in the young woman before him.

Elspeth. Cecil.

The name reverberated through Evelyn's mind, each syllable a dagger to her heart. Her gaze locked onto the girl's face, drinking in every feature with a desperate hunger. Those eyes—Archie's eyes—gazed back at her from a face that could have been her own, years ago, now.

"It's a pleasure to meet you, Miss Cecil," Edgar

said, his voice steady despite the slight tremor in his hand as he reached out to shake Elspeth's.

Evelyn's throat constricted, choking back the cry that threatened to escape. She forced her lips into a placid smile, even as her mind reeled. How could this be happening? How could her daughter—the child she had given up, the secret she had buried so deep—be standing here, in this very room?

"The pleasure is mine, Mr. Bloodworth," Elspeth replied, her voice as gentle and melodious as a spring breeze. "I've heard so much about your family's estate. It's even more magnificent than I imagined."

"*Lord* Bloodworth," Julien corrected as his chest puffed with pride. "Indeed, Miss Cecil. Bloodworth Manor has been in our family for generations. Perhaps, Edgar can give you a tour of the grounds later."

Evelyn's fingers twitched, longing to reach out and touch Elspeth, to confirm that she was real and not some cruel apparition. Instead, she took a sip of champagne, the bubbles burning her throat as she swallowed hard.

"I would be delighted," Edgar said, his eyes never leaving Elspeth's face. Yet, it was clear, at least to his mother, that his look was one of potential friendship, and nothing more. Then again, friendship would still be something more than she'd ever achieved with her own husband.

The joy of seeing her daughter, of drinking in every detail of her face and mannerisms, warred violently with the horror of what Julien was proposing. An engagement. Between siblings.

The thought made Evelyn's stomach churn.

She pressed her lips together, willing her face to remain impassive as her mind raced. How could she stop this? How could she protect both her children without revealing the truth that would destroy everything?

"Lady Bloodworth," Elspeth said shyly, turning to Evelyn with a warm smile. "It's an honour to meet you, as well. Your home is truly breathtaking."

Evelyn's heart clenched at the sound of her daughter's voice addressing her so formally. She longed to gather Elspeth in her arms; to whisper all the words of love and longing she had held back and buried deep for so many years.

Instead, she inclined her head graciously. "Thank you, Miss Cecil. We're pleased to have you here." Her voice sounded distant to her own ears, as if someone else were speaking through her.

As Julien began to regale Elspeth with tales of the manor's history, Evelyn's mind whirled with possibilities and consequences. She had to find a way to stop this engagement before it went any further. But how? And at what cost?

The weight of her secrets pressed down upon her, threatening to crush her beneath their burden. Yet as she watched Elspeth laugh at something Edgar had said, her eyes crinkling in a way that was so achingly familiar, Evelyn felt a fierce determination take root in her heart.

She would find a way. She had to. As she always did. For both her children's sakes.

Edgar leaned in slightly, his dark eyes alight with genuine interest as he addressed Elspeth. "I hear you're quite the accomplished pianist, Miss Cecil. Do you have a favourite composer?"

Elspeth's young face brightened; her delicate features animated by enthusiasm. "Oh, I adore Chopin! His nocturnes speak to my soul. And you, Lord Edgar? Are you musically inclined?"

"I'm afraid my talents lie more in the realm of literature," Edgar admitted with a self-deprecating smile. "But I'd be honoured to turn pages for you, should you wish to grace us with a performance."

As the two young people continued their exchange, finding common ground in their love of the arts, Evelyn watched from the periphery. Her eyes, usually so composed, flickered with barely concealed anguish. She clasped her hands tightly, willing them not to tremble as she observed the easy rapport developing between her children.

"They seem to be getting along splendidly," Julien murmured, appearing at her side with a satisfied smirk.

Evelyn forced a tight-lipped smile. "Indeed." She paused, gathering her courage. "If you'll excuse me, I believe I'll show Miss Cecil to the music room.

Perhaps, we can coax a performance from her, after all."

As she approached the pair, Evelyn's heart raced. "Miss Cecil," she began, her voice warm despite the turmoil within, "would you care to see our music room? I'd love to hear more about your life in London."

Elspeth's eyes lit up. "I'd be delighted, Lady Bloodworth."

As they walked, Evelyn subtly observed her daughter, drinking in every detail. "Tell me," she began carefully, "what do you enjoy most about city life?"

"The vibrancy, mostly, the constant hum of activity," Elspeth replied thoughtfully. "But also, the quiet moments—watching the sunrise over the Thames, or finding a secluded corner in a bustling park." She paused, a gentle smile playing on her lips. "My father always encouraged me to find beauty in unexpected places."

Evelyn's breath caught at the mention of her father, knowing perfectly well who her father really was, yet knowing equally as well that was not who she meant. "Your father sounds like a wise man," she managed, her voice thick with emotion, not knowing what else to say.

"He is," Elspeth agreed softly. "He taught me that true strength lies in kindness, and that empathy is the greatest virtue one can possess."

As they reached the music room, Evelyn felt her heart swell with a bittersweet mixture of pride and longing. This remarkable young woman, with her gentle spirit and innate goodness, was her daughter. And now, faced again with the seemingly impossible task of protecting both her children, Evelyn knew that her resolve would be tested like never before.

Evelyn's fingers trembled as she closed the heavy oak door of her chambers behind her, leaning against it for support. The weight of the day's revelations threatened to crush her. She crossed the room on unsteady legs, sinking onto the edge of her bed, her usually bright eyes feeling blurry and unfocused as she stared at the intricate patterns of the Persian rug beneath her feet.

"I cannot allow this to happen," she whispered fiercely, her hands clenching into fists in her lap. The image of Edgar and Elspeth together, blissfully unaware of their true connection, seared itself into her mind. Evelyn's maternal instinct roared to life, a fierce determination settling over her like armour.

Rising abruptly, she strode to the window, her reflection in the glass a portrait of resolve. *I will find a way to stop this engagement,* she vowed to herself. *For both their sakes. For all our sakes. As I have always done... and will always do.*

For that was a mother's directive.

A flicker of movement in the garden below caught her eye. Evelyn's breath hitched as she recognised Edgar and Elspeth strolling along the rose-lined path. She pressed closer to the glass, watching intently.

Edgar's head was bent towards Elspeth, a rare, unguarded smile on his face as he gestured animatedly. Elspeth's laughter drifted up, a melodious sound that tugged at Evelyn's heart. As she observed their easy companionship, a chill of dread ran down her spine.

"They're already growing close," Evelyn murmured, her brow furrowing. "I must act quickly, before it's too late."

Edgar paused to pluck a perfect red rose, presenting it to Elspeth with a gallant bow. The young woman's cheeks flushed as she accepted it, twirling the stem between her fingers.

Evelyn's hand pressed against the cool glass. "Oh, my darlings," she breathed, her voice catching. "If only you knew the truth."

The urgency of her situation crashed over her anew. Time was slipping away, each moment bringing Edgar and Elspeth closer to an engagement that could never be. Evelyn straightened her shoulders, her reflection in the window transforming into a woman of steel and fire.

"I will protect you both," she promised, her voice

barely above a whisper. "No matter the cost."

The dying light of dusk filtered through the heavy curtains, casting long shadows across Evelyn's chamber. Her eyes, bright with determination, darted from corner to corner as she paced the length of her room. The soft rustle of her skirts against the rug was the only sound breaking the tense silence.

"There must be a way," Evelyn muttered, her fingers twisting anxiously. "Something I can do without revealing everything..."

She paused by her writing desk, her gaze falling on a framed portrait of Edgar as a child. His kind eyes and gentle smile tugged at her heart, strengthening her resolve.

"No," she said firmly, squaring her shoulders. "I cannot protect him with half-truths any longer. Edgar deserves to know everything."

The weight of her decision settled upon her; heavy, yet oddly freeing. Evelyn took a deep breath, steeling herself for what was to come.

As the last rays of sunlight faded, Evelyn slipped from her room into the dimly lit corridor. The usual bustling activity of Bloodworth Manor had quieted, leaving an eerie stillness in its wake. Her footsteps, muffled by the thick scarlet runners, seemed thunderous in the silence.

Portraits of stern-faced Bloodworth ancestors

watched her passage, their painted eyes seeming to follow her every move. Evelyn's heart raced, but she pressed on, drawing strength from the love that drove her forward.

At last, she reached Edgar's door. Evelyn hesitated, her hand hovering over the ornate handle. "For both my children," she whispered, a prayer and a promise. With a deep breath, she knocked softly, prepared to change the course of their lives forever.

Edgar's door creaked open, revealing his surprised face. "Mother? Is everything alright?"

Evelyn stepped inside, her deep green eyes meeting her son's concerned gaze. "Edgar, my dear, we need to talk."

The room was bathed in the warm glow of a single lamp, casting long shadows across Edgar's features. He gestured to a pair of chairs by the fireplace, his brow furrowed with worry.

As they sat, Evelyn's hands trembled slightly. She clasped them tightly in her lap, willing herself to find the right words. "Edgar, what I'm about to tell you... it will change everything. But you must know the truth."

Edgar leaned forward, his voice gentle. "Mother, whatever it is, you can tell me."

Evelyn took a deep breath, her voice wavering. "Elspeth... she's not just Lord Cecil's daughter. The truth is that she was adopted as a baby, by the Cecils."

"Mother, that doesn't bother me at all. She seems like a lovely woman. I know father would not approve, if he knew, but we don't have to tell him."

"No, my dear," she shook her head lightly, trying to pretend she didn't have to say what she did. "She's not only adopted... She's... she's your half-sister."

Edgar's eyes widened in shock. "What? But how... ?"

"Many years ago, when you were just an infant, I... I had an affair with Archibald Bates," Evelyn confessed, her words tumbling out in a rush. "Elspeth is the result of that union."

Edgar sat back, stunned into silence. Evelyn watched him anxiously, her heart pounding. She could see the emotions flickering across his face—disbelief, confusion, and then a dawning understanding.

"Uncle Archie... All these years," Edgar murmured, his voice barely above a whisper. "You've carried this secret alone?"

Evelyn nodded, tears welling in her eyes. "I had to protect you both. But now, with this engagement... I couldn't let it continue without you knowing the truth."

Edgar's expression softened, and he reached out

to take his mother's hand. "Oh, Mother," he said, his voice filled with empathy. "What a burden you've borne."

Evelyn felt a wave of relief wash over her. "You're not... angry with me?"

"Angry? No," Edgar replied, shaking his head. "Surprised, yes. But I understand why you kept this secret. The consequences if it were known..."

"Would be catastrophic," Evelyn finished, her voice regaining some of its usual strength. "For all of us."

Edgar nodded, his mind clearly racing. "We must find a way to stop this engagement without revealing the truth. But how?"

Evelyn squeezed his hand, her heart swelling with love and gratitude for her son's understanding. "We'll find a way, together. Thank you, Edgar, for your compassion."

As they sat in the flickering firelight, mother and son united by their shared secret, Evelyn felt a glimmer of hope. The road ahead would be challenging, but with Edgar by her side, she felt stronger than ever before.

Edgar's shoulders tensed, his gaze dropping to their intertwined hands. "Mother, I... I have a confession of my own," he said, his voice quavering. Evelyn's heart quickened, sensing the weight of his words.

"What is it, darling?" she asked gently, stroking his hand with her thumb.

Edgar took a deep breath, his dark green eyes—so like her own—meeting hers with trepidation. "I've never felt... drawn to women. My heart, it..." he paused, swallowing hard. "It yearns for the company of men."

Evelyn's breath caught in her throat, understanding dawning. "Oh, Edgar," she whispered.

"Father would be furious if he knew," Edgar continued, his voice barely audible. "I've been so afraid, mother. Afraid of disappointing him, of disappointing you, of being cast out..."

Evelyn cupped her son's face in her hands, her eyes brimming with tears. "My darling boy, you could never disappoint me. Your happiness is all that matters."

Edgar's shoulders sagged with relief, years of tension melting away. "You... you accept me?"

"With all my heart," Evelyn replied fiercely, pulling him into a tight embrace. Edgar clung to her, his body shaking with silent sobs.

As they held each other, Evelyn's mind raced. This changed everything—and yet, nothing at all. Their mission remained the same: to protect Elspeth and prevent the engagement. But now, they were bound by more than just blood; they were united by their secrets, their fears, and their unwavering love for each other.

"We'll face this together," Evelyn murmured into Edgar's hair. "You and I, we'll find a way through this maze. No matter what comes, we have each other."

Edgar pulled back, wiping his eyes. A small, grateful smile played on his lips. "Thank you, mother. I never imagined... never dared to hope for such acceptance."

Evelyn's heart swelled with fierce pride and love for her son.

"You are perfect as you are, Edgar. Never doubt that. And together, we will protect Elspeth and forge a path forward—for all of us."

Evelyn's eyes darted to the flickering candle on Edgar's bedside table, its flame casting dancing shadows across the room. She leaned closer, her voice dropping to a whisper. "We must act swiftly, but with caution. The engagement cannot proceed, yet we cannot risk exposing our secrets."

Edgar nodded; his brow furrowed in concentration. "Perhaps, we could... create a distraction? Something to draw attention away from the betrothal?"

"No," Evelyn shook her head, her eyes glinting with determination. "It must be more subtle. We need to plant seeds of doubt, make them question the match without arousing suspicion."

Edgar's fingers drummed against his knee as he contemplated. "What if I were to express reservations about marriage? Cite a desire to travel, to see the world before settling down?"

A small smile tugged at Evelyn's lips. "That could work. And I could hint at concerns about Elspeth's youth, her readiness for such a commitment."

"But Father..." Edgar's voice trailed off, his earlier vulnerability resurfacing.

Evelyn reached out, squeezing his hand. "Leave your father to me. I've navigated his moods for years. I know I was younger than Elspeth when we married, but times have changed. Trust me, darling."

Edgar exhaled slowly, his shoulders relaxing. "It won't be easy, will it?"

"No," Evelyn admitted, her tone gentle but resolute. "But we'll face whatever comes together. Our love—for each other, for Elspeth, will guide us through."

As she rose to leave, Edgar caught her hand. "Mother, I... thank you. For everything."

Evelyn's heart swelled with affection. She bent to kiss his forehead, murmuring, "Always, my darling boy. Always."

Chapter 14

Julien's Wrath

The heavy ticking of the grandfather clock echoed through Julien's study, matching the rhythmic tap of his polished shoes on the hardwood floor. His steely eyes narrowed as he paced, hands clasped tightly behind his back. Edgar's defiance burned in his mind, a festering wound to his authority.

"Impertinent boy," Julien muttered, his voice as cold as the winter wind howling outside. "There must be more to this refusal."

He paused at the window, gazing out at the snow-covered grounds of Bloodworth Manor. The white expanse seemed to mock him, hiding secrets beneath its pristine surface.

Just like this family, Julien thought bitterly.

A sharp knock interrupted his brooding. "Enter," he commanded.

The butler appeared from behind the heavy

doorframe, a silver tray in hand. "Your afternoon correspondence, my lord." He droned, his voice as grey and icy as the frost that clung to the windows, as if his very being reflected little but a monotone existence.

Taking the bundle of letters, Julien ruffled through them with a dismissive speed before his attention was caught by a particular envelope, addressed not to him, but to Evelyn. His jaw clenched as he waved the butler away before hastily beginning to unfold the already smudged page between his thick fingers.

Who could possibly be writing to her?

As his dark eyes quickly scanned over the words in front of him, the fury built hot and fast within him.

"My dearest Evelyn," he read aloud, his voice dripping with venom. "I write only to say how deeply I miss you, how I miss our evenings under the stars..."

He stopped dead. The letter slipped from his grasp, fluttering to the floor like a fallen leaf. Julien's mind raced, piecing together the implications of this betrayal. Evelyn, his wife, in league with that charming rogue, Archie.

"That conniving bitch!" he growled, slamming his fist onto the mahogany desk, the reverberations causing the crystal glasses perched in the old liquor cabinet to tinkle violently.

"Nothing but a common whore, a selfish wench who should have learnt her place year ago. I will *not* allow this scandal to taint the Bloodworth name."

He strode over to the cabinet, pouring himself a generous measure of brandy. As the amber liquid burned down his throat, Julien's icy demeanour returned. He would unravel this web of lies, no matter the cost.

The heavy oak door of Evelyn's chambers crashed open, the sound reverberating through the room like a thunderclap. Julien strode in, his tall frame filling the doorway, eyes glinting with barely contained fury.

Evelyn rose from her dressing table, her eyes meeting his in the mirror. She turned slowly, her chin raised in defiance despite the tremor in her hands. "Julien," she said, her voice steady. "What is the meaning of this intrusion?"

"Silence!" Julien's voice cut through the air like a whip. "Your deceit ends now, Evelyn. I know everything."

Evelyn's heart raced, but she stood her ground, years of quiet resilience fortifying her resolve. She thought of Elspeth, of the need to protect her at all costs. Of her song. Of Archie. And of herself. "I'm afraid I don't understand, my lord," she replied, her tone measured.

Julien advanced, his face a mask of cold rage. "Do

not play the fool with me. Your affair with Archie, did you think I wouldn't discover your betrayal?"

Evelyn's mind whirled. How had he uncovered their secret? She steeled herself, knowing the danger that lay ahead. "Julien, please... it was years ago," she began, her voice barely above a whisper. "Let me explain—"

But she knew she could never explain.

"Explain?" Julien spat, his words dripping with venom. "Explain how you've made a mockery of our marriage? How you've tainted the Bloodworth name with your indiscretions?"

Evelyn's fists clenched at her sides. She thought of the years of isolation, of Julien's cold indifference, of Archie's warmth and kindness. "You speak of betrayal," she said, her voice gaining strength, "but what of your own actions? The neglect, the cruelty—"

"Enough!" Julien spat, closing the distance between them. "You will pay for this, I swear it."

And with that, he stormed from the room, leaving Evelyn reeling with the thought of his threats.

An hour later, Julien found himself sitting back at his mahogany desk, his fingers steepled beneath his chin as he contemplated his next move. The ticking of the grandfather clock punctuated the oppressive silence of his study. His steely eyes narrowed as he reached for a sheet of pristine stationery.

"Archie, my dear cousin," he murmured, his pen scratching across the paper. "How long has it been since we've enjoyed each other's company?"

He paused, a cold smile playing at the corners of his mouth. "Yes, a family gathering is long overdue. And what better occasion than to celebrate young Edgar's upcoming nuptials?"

As he sealed the envelope, Julien's thoughts turned to Evelyn and her confession. His jaw clenched. "You've made a grave mistake, my dear," he muttered. "But I will see order restored to this house."

Three days later, the iron gates of Bloodworth Manor creaked open, admitting a carriage bearing Archie Bates. As he stepped onto the gravel drive for the first time in almost twenty years, Archie's usual carefree demeanour faltered. The manor loomed before him, its windows like watchful eyes, the stone façade cold and uninviting.

"Well, old girl," Archie said, patting the carriage door, "you're looking as cheerful as ever."

The footman who greeted him remained stoic. "The Marquis sends his regards, but finds himself currently engaged. He will be meeting you in the drawing room in the morning to greet you properly, himself."

Archie nodded, forcing a smile. "Ah, I do hope Julien's mellowed since our last encounter. Though I suspect the chances of that are about as likely as this place sprouting daffodils from its foundations."

The evening seemed to pass in a blur of swirling thoughts, and it felt like no time had passed by the time the grandfather clock in the hallway chimed midnight, its sonorous tones echoing through the dimly lit corridor. Archie, unable to sleep—his mind caught up in wonderings about Evelyn, and when he might see her during his visit—had ventured out for a late-night stroll. As he rounded the corner, he came face to face with Julien, whose imposing figure seemed to materialise from the shadows, as if stepping out from the dark walls of the manor itself.

"Ah, cousin!" Archie exclaimed, his voice carrying a forced cheerfulness. "I thought I was not to see you until tomorrow, but it seems midnight wanderings are to be a family trait. Shall we raid the kitchens together? I've heard tales of your cook's legendary midnight puddings."

Julien's steely gaze fixed on Archie, his eyes glinting dangerously in the flickering candlelight. The acrid smell of brandy hung in the air between them.

"Your levity is misplaced, Archie," Julien growled, his words clipped and precise despite his inebriated state. "We have matters of grave importance to discuss."

Archie's smile faltered, but he pressed on. "Come now, Julien. Surely nothing's so dire it can't wait until morning? A good night's rest often brings clarity to even the most troubling—"

"Silence!" Julien thundered, his commanding presence filling the narrow space. "Your silver tongue will not serve you here. I know of your... indiscretions with my wife."

Archie's heart raced, his mind whirling. How could Julien possibly know? He forced a laugh, though it sounded hollow even to his own ears. "My dear cousin, I fear you've had one brandy too many. Evelyn and I are merely—"

"Do not insult my intelligence," Julien snarled, advancing on Archie. "Your lies are as transparent as they are despicable."

Archie raised his hands in a placating gesture, backing away. "Julien, please. Let's discuss this rationally. There's been a misunderstanding—"

But Julien's rage had reached its boiling point. With a roar of fury, he lunged at Archie, his fists connecting with a sickening thud. Archie stumbled, his back hitting the wall as he desperately tried to fend off Julien's assault.

"Julien, stop!" Archie gasped, tasting blood as his face began to ache with a dull pain. "This madness solves nothing!"

As the two men grappled in the shadowy hallway, Archie's thoughts raced. How had it come to this? And more pressingly, how could he diffuse this situation before it spiralled beyond control?

Julien's eyes flashed with a cold, murderous glint as he seized Archie by the lapels. "You've brought this upon yourself," he hissed, his breath hot with the stench of brandy.

In one swift, terrible motion, Julien shoved Archie with all his might. Time seemed to slow as Archie teetered at the top of the grand staircase, his arms windmilling desperately. For a heartbeat, their eyes locked—Archie's wide with disbelief, Julien's narrowed with glacial contempt.

Then, with a sickening lurch, Archie plummeted backwards. The ornate banister rushed past in a blur as he tumbled down the sweeping stairs. Each impact sent shockwaves of pain throughout his body, the dull thuds echoing through the cavernous foyer.

"Julien!" Archie cried out, his voice strangled with panic and pain. But there was no response, only the terrible finality of his own body crashing against the marble floor below.

A deafening silence fell over Bloodworth Manor.

Julien stood motionless at the top of the stairs, his chest heaving. He stared down at

Archie's crumpled form, a pool of crimson slowly spreading beneath his cousin's golden hair.

"An unfortunate accident," he muttered, descending the stairs with measured steps. "Nothing more."

Kneeling beside Archie's lifeless body, Julien's hands moved with practiced efficiency. He adjusted Archie's limbs, arranging them in a macabre tableau of a drunken fall. His fingers deftly plucked a half-empty brandy snifter from a nearby table, placing it near Archie's outstretched hand.

"You always did enjoy your spirits a bit too much, dear cousin," Julien remarked, his tone almost conversational. "It was bound to lead to tragedy sooner or later."

∞∞∞

Evelyn's fingers trembled as she listened to the words coming from Florence's mouth. The world blurred before her eyes, but the words were seared into her heart: Archie, dead. A fall. An accident.

"No," she whispered, her eyes wide with disbelief. "It can't be."

She stumbled to the window, desperate for air. The manicured gardens of Bloodworth Manor stretched before her, a cruel mockery of tranquillity. Her mind raced, recalling Julien's icy demeanour, his thinly veiled threats.

"My lady..." Florence started, taking a step towards her mistress, wanting nothing more than to comfort her, but not knowing how.

"Oh, God, Archie," Evelyn breathed, not even hearing her handmaid from behind her, but only a high-pitched screaming in her ears. She pressed a hand to her mouth to stifle a sob. "What has he done to you?"

The weight of realisation crashed over her like a tidal wave. Julien knew. He had discovered their affair, he had warned her, and now Archie... Her lover, her confidant, her beacon of warmth in this cold manor, this cold world, was gone forever.

Evelyn's gaze fell upon a portrait of her son, his innocent face beaming up at her. A chill ran down her spine as she considered his fate. Considered Elspeth's fate. If Julien could do this to his own cousin, what wouldn't he do to protect his legacy?

"I won't let him harm them," she vowed, her voice barely above a whisper. "I can't."

Her fingers clenched into fists, nails biting into her palms. The pain grounded her, cleared her mind. Evelyn took a deep, steadying breath, feeling a steely resolve settle over her like armour.

With a deep breath, she turned to the woman behind her. "You can go now, Florence."

"But Evelyn—"

"I said go!" The words left her mouth far harsher than she had intended, but she needed to be alone, to process all she'd been told.

Florence bowed her head lightly, leaving Evelyn and her grief alone together. "Yes, Lady Bloodworth."

Just as the door closed behind the housemaid, a deafening scream escaped from Evelyn's dry lips as a waterfall of tears burst free from their holding place at the corner of her eyes. Her chest heaved as she tried her hardest to intake breath, failing drastically at this quest, the squeals of her hysteric screaming mixing with the harsh rasps of her dying breath, as she began to hyperventilate.

Pain struck throughout her body as she continued trying her hardest to breathe, the salty water falling from her eyes landing in her mouth. There was no way to describe it, no way to comprehend what she felt. How alone and empty she was.

And then the world went silent, there was nothing left but the ringing in her ears. The screams had ceased, the rasps of breath had gone, and she was left with only the eeriness of the air surrounding her at all angles. Suddenly, she felt nothing. Everything seemed so blank, so devoid of any emotion, so desolate.

Chapter 14

The Final Confrontation

The polished wooden floors of Bloodworth Manor's dining room echoed with Evelyn's measured footsteps as she entered, her eyes scanning the opulent space. Her heart raced beneath the calm exterior she'd carefully constructed; each beat a reminder of the gravity of what was to come.

"You can do this," she thought, steadying her breath. "For Edgar, for Elspeth, for yourself."

The heavy oak door creaked open, and Marquis Julien Bloodworth's imposing figure filled the frame. His steely gaze swept the room before settling on Evelyn, and the air seemed to chill in his wake.

Evelyn's spine stiffened instinctively, but she forced a placid smile. "Good evening, my lord," she said, her voice a study in measured elegance. "I trust your day has been productive?"

Julien's lip curled slightly as he strode to the head of the table. "Productivity is the hallmark of a Bloodworth, is it not?" His tone carried the weight of expectation, of judgment.

"Indeed," Evelyn replied, her fingers ghosting over the back of her chair. She watched as Julien took his seat, his movements precise and controlled. The candles flickered, casting dancing shadows across his sharp features.

"I've been considering Edgar's future," Evelyn ventured, her words carefully chosen. She lowered herself into her chair, arranging her skirts with deliberate grace. "Perhaps, it's time we discussed his education in more detail."

Julien's eyes narrowed almost imperceptibly. "The boy's future is not your concern, Evelyn. I've made my plans clear, for his education, for his upcoming marriage to Miss Cecil."

Evelyn's heart clenched, but she maintained her composure.

"As his mother, I believe I have some say in the matter," she countered, her voice soft but firm.

The tension in the room thickened, nearly palpable. Julien's hand tightened around his crystal goblet, and Evelyn found herself wondering if he could sense the shift in her demeanour, the quiet rebellion brewing beneath her carefully cultivated façade.

"You forget your place," Julien said, his words clipped and cold. "In this house, in this family, there is only one voice that matters."

Evelyn met his gaze, unflinching.

Perhaps it's time for that to change, she thought, but aloud she simply said, "I understand, my lord. I merely wish to ensure the best for our son."

As the first course was served, Evelyn's mind raced with the weight of her plans, of the secrets she carried. She watched Julien from beneath lowered lashes, noting every movement, every nuance. The game had begun, and she was determined to see it through to its bitter end.

The aroma of roasted pheasant wafted through the air, a stark contrast to the acrid tension that hung between them. Evelyn's gaze swept over the opulent spread—crystal goblets catching the candlelight, fine china adorned with intricate gold filigree, and silverware that gleamed like newly minted coins. Yet, despite the sumptuous feast before her, her appetite had abandoned her entirely.

"I've been thinking," Evelyn began, her voice steady despite the tumult in her chest, "about Edgar's interests in literature and philosophy. Perhaps, a term at Oxford would suit him well."

Julien's fork paused midway to his mouth, his steely eyes locking onto hers. "Oxford? Nonsense. The boy will learn the management of our estates, as is his duty."

Evelyn took a measured sip of wine, buying herself a moment. In her mind, she saw Edgar's crestfallen face when Julien had last crushed his dreams. She pressed on, "But surely a well-rounded education would only enhance his ability to manage the estates? The connections he could make—"

"Enough," Julien cut her off, his tone brooking no argument. "You coddle the boy too much, Evelyn. It's high time he learnt his place in this family and took his bride, as is his duty."

The words *his place* echoed in Evelyn's mind; a grim reminder of the oppressive control Julien wielded over them all. She felt a flicker of defiance ignite within her.

"And what place is that, my lord?" she asked, her striking green eyes meeting his unflinchingly. "To be another pawn in your grand design?"

Julien's expression darkened, a storm gathering in his gaze. "Watch your tongue, madam. You tread on dangerous ground."

Evelyn's heart raced, but she pressed on, each word carefully chosen. "I only wish for our child to have the freedom to pursue his passions, to live life unburdened by… excessive expectations."

As Julien's jaw clenched, Evelyn saw a flash of the man she'd once feared so deeply. But now, with her resolve hardened by years of silent suffering, she found strength in her purpose. The die was cast, and there was no turning back now.

Evelyn's gaze never wavered as she continued, her voice steady. "Do you remember the day you locked Edgar in his room for a week because he dared to express interest in art? Or when you denied him his favourite toy simply because he spoke out of turn at dinner?"

Julien's lip curled in dismissal, his arrogance seeping from the cracks in his greying moustache. "Discipline is necessary for proper upbringing, my dear. You're far too soft-hearted to understand such matters."

"Discipline?" Evelyn almost scoffed, her tone laced with quiet fury. "Is that what you called it when you had the gardener's son whipped for accidentally trampling your prized roses?"

A flicker of unease crossed Julien's face, quickly masked by contempt. "Peasants must learn their place. It's the natural order of things. Bloodworth Manor is known and revered for its scarlet roses and ivy; we couldn't have them crushed like a common insect. No, not the very symbols of this great house."

Evelyn leaned forward, her emerald eyes blazing with newfound defiance. "And what of the dungeon beneath the east wing? Is that part of your *natural order* as well, Julien? Because, from what I hear, the disgusting things you get up to down there are anything but natural."

The words hung in the air like a thunderclap. Julien's face drained of colour, his composure cracking for the first time. "How did you—" he began, then caught himself, rage simmering beneath his aristocratic veneer.

Evelyn's heart pounded, a mix of fear and exhilaration coursing through her veins. She thought, *This is it. There's no going back now.*

Aloud, she pressed on, "I know everything, Julien. Every dark secret, every cruel act. Your reign of terror ends tonight."

Julien's face contorted with fury, his mask of civility shattering entirely. He slammed his fist on the table, causing the fine china to rattle. "You insolent wench!" he roared, rising to his full height. "How dare you speak to me in such a manner? I am the Marquis of Bloodworth, and you are nothing but a simpering child I foolishly took as a wife!"

Evelyn flinched inwardly at his outburst, but outwardly remained still as stone, her eyes never leaving his. She thought, *He's like a wounded animal now, dangerous but weakening.* Her voice, when she spoke, was calm and steady. "Your title means nothing in the face of your cruelty, Julien. It cannot protect you from the truth."

Julien's hand shot out, grasping her wrist with

bruising force. "I will not be threatened in my own home," he hissed, his face inches from hers. "Perhaps, it's time I reminded you of your place, my dear."

Evelyn's heart raced, but she did not cower. Instead, she met his gaze unflinchingly. "There is nothing more you can do to me, Julien. I am no longer afraid of you."

With a snarl of frustration, Julien released her, taking a step back and reaching for his wine glass. As he brought it to his lips, Evelyn felt a surge of satisfaction mingled with fear. She watched him intently, her outward calm belying the tumult of emotions within.

It's done, she thought, her pulse quickening. *There's no turning back now.* A potent mix of anticipation and dread coursed through her veins as she observed Julien take a long drink.

"You may think you've won some small victory here," Julien sneered, oblivious to what he had just consumed. "But remember this, Evelyn, I still hold all the power. Your pathetic attempts at rebellion will only bring you more suffering. The dungeon, as you put it, has plenty of open space for such insolent women."

Evelyn's lips curved into a small, enigmatic smile. "We shall see," she replied softly, her words heavy with unspoken meaning. "We shall see."

Julien's brow furrowed, his hand trembling as

he set down the wine glass. "What... what have you done?" he slurred, his normally piercing gaze growing unfocused.

Evelyn's heart thundered in her chest as she watched him, her blazing eyes never leaving his face. "Nothing you haven't brought upon yourself, Julien," she said, her voice steady despite the maelstrom of emotions within her.

The Marquis attempted to take a step toward her, his movements uncoordinated and sluggish. He grasped the edge of the table, knuckles white with effort. "You treacherous witch," he spat, but the words lacked their usual venom.

Evelyn rose gracefully, her composure a stark contrast to Julien's deteriorating state. "For years, I've endured your cruelty," she said, her tone laced with quiet determination. "But no more. You've underestimated me for the last time. You know I've always loved my garden. The red roses, the vibrant tulips... the beautiful violet of the belladonna."

As Julien swayed on his feet, Evelyn stepped closer, her voice dropping to a near whisper. "There's something you should know about Elspeth," she began, savouring the moment she'd long dreamed of. "She isn't just some stranger from the city. Haven't you noticed the familiarity in her eyes?"

The revelation hit Julien like a physical blow. He

staggered back, confusion and rage warring in his glassy eyes. "Impossible," he growled, but doubt had already taken root.

"She is the product of a love you could never understand," Evelyn continued, her words carrying the weight of years of secrecy. "A love born of kindness and compassion, not duty and fear."

Julien's face contorted in fury, but his weakened state rendered him impotent. Evelyn watched as the realisation dawned on him, shattering the façade of control he'd clung to for so long.

This is it, Evelyn thought, a mix of triumph and sorrow washing over her. *The end of his tyranny, the beginning of our freedom.*

Evelyn's emerald eyes locked onto Julien's fading gaze, her heart racing with a mixture of fear and resolve. She drew a deep breath, steeling herself for the final revelation.

"And there's more," she said, her voice steady despite the trembling in her hands. "Our beloved son, Edgar—the child you've long considered the pinnacle of the Bloodworth legacy—he too holds a secret that would shatter your world."

Julien's bloodshot eyes widened, his lips working soundlessly as he struggled to form words. Evelyn pressed on, her tone softening with a hint of compassion for her son, as she leant close to the Marquis' face and whispered, "Edgar's heart belongs not to any woman, but to those of men. He's known this truth about himself for years, living in fear of your judgment and cruelty... but not anymore."

A guttural sound escaped Julien's throat, a noise caught between a groan and a roar. He lurched forward, grasping at the edge of the dining table for support, as Evelyn leant back to avoid him.

"No," he rasped, his once-commanding voice reduced to a hoarse whisper as a foam began to collect around his bluing lips. "You lie!"

Evelyn shook her head slowly, a sad smile playing at the corners of her lips. "I speak only the truth, Julien. The legacy you've fought so hard to protect crumbles around you."

She watched as the last vestiges of Julien's authority drained from his face, replaced by a mask of despair and disbelief. His imposing frame seemed to shrink before her eyes, the poison of the deadly nightshade and revelations working in tandem to destroy him.

How small he looks now, Evelyn thought, a pang of pity cutting through her resolve. *A man undone by his own hatred.*

Julien's legs gave way, and he collapsed to the floor, gasping for air. Evelyn stood over him, her expression a complex mixture of emotions—relief, sadness, and an overwhelming sense of finality.

"Eve... lyn," Julien choked out, his steely eyes now clouded and unfocused. "How... dare... you..."

She knelt beside him, close enough to hear his laboured breathing but just out of reach. "It's over, Julien," she whispered. "Your reign of terror ends here."

As the light faded from Julien's eyes, Evelyn felt the weight of years lifting from her shoulders. She watched the life drain from the man who had controlled her existence for so long, her heart heavy with the knowledge of what she had done, yet buoyed by the promise of freedom.

As Julien's final breath escaped his foaming lips, a profound silence settled over the dining room. Evelyn rose slowly, her eyes fixed on the still form of her husband. The oppressive atmosphere that had permeated Bloodworth Manor for so long seemed to dissipate, leaving her feeling lighter than she had in years.

"It's done," she whispered to herself, her voice trembling slightly. "It's finally over."

Evelyn's gaze swept across the opulent room, taking in the ornate furnishings and gleaming silverware that had once felt like gilded bars of a cage. Now, they seemed powerless, mere relics of a tyranny overthrown.

She walked to the grand windows, pulling back the heavy curtains to let the moonlight flood in. The grounds of Bloodworth Manor stretched before her, bathed in a silvery glow that felt symbolic of her newfound freedom.

What have I become? Evelyn mused, her reflection ghostly in the windowpane. *A murderer? A liberator? Perhaps both.*

Her thoughts turned to Edgar, and a small smile tugged at her lips. *My dear boy, you'll never have to fear him again. You can be who you truly are now.*

With a deep breath, Evelyn straightened her posture, feeling the strength that had always resided within her surge to the forefront. She turned back to face the room, her eyes blazing with determination.

"This is *my* home now," she declared to the empty space. "And I will reshape it as I see fit."

As she strode towards the door, each step felt like a reclamation. The shadows that had once threatened to engulf her now seemed to retreat, cowed by her newfound authority.

Evelyn paused at the threshold, her hand on the doorknob. "I was once a frightened girl, thrown into a life I didn't choose," she murmured. "But now, I am Lady Appleby Bloodworth in more than just name. And I will use this power to protect those I love."

And she couldn't help but wonder if she had not been in his hands, if she had not been stuck under his large, imposing thumb, that maybe she may have bloomed, maybe she would have grown into a wildflower, a rich rose; crimson, strong, and riddled with thorns.

With a final glance at Julien's lifeless form, Evelyn stepped into the hallway, ready to face the future she had fought so hard to secure. The oppressive weight of Bloodworth Manor's shadows had lifted, and in its place, a world of possibilities awaited.

Chapter 16

Aftermath and Revelations

The grand hall of Bloodworth Manor loomed before Evelyn, its vaulted ceilings and ornate tapestries now feeling so different than they ever had before. The weight of Julien's death hung in the air, a discernible tension that seemed to cling to every surface. Evelyn's eyes swept across the polished marble floor, her reflection a ghostly echo of the woman she once was.

She inhaled deeply, her chest tightening as she steeled herself for what lay ahead. The staff would be gathering soon, their faces etched with a mixture of fear and uncertainty. How would they react to the news? Would they believe the story of Julien's sudden seizure, or would suspicion linger in their eyes?

Evelyn's fingers brushed against the cool surface of a nearby column, seeking strength from its unyielding presence. "I can do this," she whispered to herself, her voice barely audible in the cavernous space. "For Edgar, for the staff, for myself."

As if summoned by her thoughts, Edgar appeared by her side, his kind eyes searching her face. "Mother," he said softly, "are you ready?"

Evelyn turned to her son, a small smile gracing her lips. "As ready as I'll ever be, my dear. Let us face this together."

With a nod, Edgar offered his arm, and they made their way to the drawing room. The staff had already assembled, their hushed whispers falling silent as Evelyn and Edgar entered. Evelyn's gaze swept across the room, taking in the familiar faces of those who had served under Julien's iron fist for so long.

Clearing her throat, Evelyn stepped forward, her voice steady and clear as she began to address the gathered crowd. "My dear friends and loyal staff of Bloodworth Manor, I stand before you today with a heavy heart but a hopeful spirit."

She paused, allowing her words to settle in the room. The eyes of those looking back were fixed upon her, a mixture of curiosity and apprehension evident in their expressions.

"As you all know, Lord Bloodworth passed away last night during our dinner from a violent fit. It was sudden and unexpected; a cruel reminder of how fragile life can be." Evelyn's mind raced, carefully choosing her next words. "With his passing, a new chapter begins for Bloodworth Manor—one of change and, I hope, of healing."

A murmur rippled through the crowd, and Evelyn felt Edgar's reassuring presence beside her. She continued, her voice gaining strength with each word. "The oppressive rule that has governed this house for so long ends today. I stand before you not just as Lady Bloodworth, but as someone who understands the hardships you have endured."

Evelyn's eyes met those of Maggie, the housekeeper who had shown her kindness when she first arrived as a young bride. The older woman's eyes glistened with unshed tears, and Evelyn felt a surge of determination.

"Changes will be made," Evelyn declared, her tone leaving no room for doubt. "Your lives and working conditions will improve. This manor will become a place of respect, fairness, and dignity for all who reside within its walls."

As she spoke, Evelyn could feel the atmosphere in the room shifting. The tension that had gripped the staff began to dissolve, replaced by a cautious hope. She saw shoulders straighten, chins lift, and even a few tentative smiles emerge.

"I know this transition may not be easy," Evelyn admitted, her voice softening. "But I ask for your trust and your patience as we work together to create a better future for Bloodworth Manor. My son, Edgar, and I are committed to this new path, and we welcome your input and ideas."

Edgar stepped forward then, his presence a testament to the unity of their vision. "We stand before you not as your masters, but as your allies," he added, his voice carrying the same quiet determination that Evelyn felt in her heart.

As Evelyn concluded her address, a sense of lightness washed over her. The weight of secrecy and fear that had burdened her for so long began to lift. She saw it reflected in the faces of the staff—a glimmer of hope, a spark of possibility.

In that moment, standing in the drawing room of Bloodworth Manor, Evelyn felt the first true stirrings of freedom. The path ahead would be challenging, but with Edgar by her side and the support of those around her, she knew they could forge a new legacy for Bloodworth Manor—one built on compassion, integrity, and hope.

The heavy oak door of Julien's study creaked open as Evelyn and Edgar entered, the scent of leather-bound books and aged parchment enveloping them. Evelyn's bright irises scanned the room, settling on the imposing mahogany desk where her late husband had orchestrated his cruel schemes.

"We must act swiftly," Evelyn said, her voice low but resolute as she approached the desk. "Those poor women have suffered enough."

Edgar nodded, his kind expression tinged with determination. "Where do we begin, Mother?"

Evelyn's slender fingers traced the outline of an ornate silver key on the desk. "This opens the bottom drawer. Your father kept his most sensitive documents there."

As she turned the key, Edgar leaned in, his brow furrowed. "I always suspected there was more to Father's business dealings, but this..."

The drawer slid open, revealing a stack of ledgers and loose papers. Evelyn's heart raced as she began sifting through them.

"Edgar, look at this," she gasped, holding up a sheet covered in names and figures. "These must be records of the women he... acquired."

Edgar's face paled. "How could he do this? How could we not have known?"

Evelyn's hand trembled slightly as she set down the paper, not having the strength to admit that she'd known for years, she'd just been too frightened to say or do anything. "We knew enough to fear him, my dear. But now, we have the power to make this right."

They worked in silence for several minutes,

organising the documents into piles. Evelyn's mind whirled with each new revelation, her resolve strengthening with every piece of evidence of Julien's cruelty.

"We'll need to contact the authorities," Edgar said, breaking the silence. "But first, we must free them ourselves."

Evelyn nodded, her eyes flashing with determination. "Yes. I'll go to them now. They deserve to hear the news from me personally."

As she stood, Edgar grasped her hand. "Mother, are you certain? Perhaps, I should—"

"No, Edgar," Evelyn interrupted gently. "This is my responsibility. Your father's actions may have been beyond my control, but I will not shy away from righting his wrongs."

With a deep breath, Evelyn made her way to the hidden chamber, her heart pounding with each step. As she entered, she was met with the sight of dimly lit torches casting dancing shadows on the damp stone walls. The faces of half a dozen women were illuminated, each one bearing the marks of fear and uncertainty etched onto their features. Their clothes were tattered and dirty, evidence of their captivity.

The chamber was a dismal place, with damp walls covered in grime and low lighting that cast a sickly yellow glow. The shadows seemed to dance and shift, making the space feel claustrophobic and eerie. A musty smell lingered in the air, and dust particles danced in the dim light. Her heart thumped in her chest as she surveyed the room, taking in the sight of the women huddled together in fear, their eyes filled with desperation and uncertainty.

"Ladies," Evelyn began, her voice steady despite the emotion threatening to overwhelm her. "I come to you with news of your freedom. Lord Bloodworth is dead, and his reign of terror ends today."

A collective gasp filled the chamber, followed by murmurs of disbelief and hope. Evelyn moved among them, unlocking their shackles one by one, her touch gentle and her words soothing.

To a frail young woman with haunted eyes, she whispered, "You're safe now. We'll provide you with everything you need to start anew."

Another, even younger woman grasped Evelyn's hand. "Why are you doing this, m'lady?"

Evelyn's eyes welled with tears, realising for the first time just how much these women had been broken down by her husband. "Because it's the right thing to do. Because you deserve your freedom and your dignity. Because I should have done it years ago."

As the last lock clicked open, Evelyn stood in the centre of the room, surrounded by the women she had liberated. The weight of their gazes upon her was both a burden and a balm.

"I cannot undo the harm that has been done to you," she said, her voice thick with emotion. "But I swear to you, on my life and on the future of Bloodworth Manor, that you will have every resource at our disposal to rebuild your lives. You are not alone on this journey."

As the women embraced each other, some weeping openly, others still in shock, Evelyn felt a profound shift within herself. The timid young bride who had first entered Bloodworth Manor was gone. In her place stood a woman of strength and purpose, ready to face the challenges ahead and forge a new legacy of compassion and justice.

∞∞∞

The flickering candlelight cast long shadows across the library's mahogany shelves as Evelyn sank into a plush armchair, her eyes reflecting the dancing flames. Edgar stood by the window, his silhouette framed against the fading twilight.

"Mother," Edgar began, his voice soft but resolute, "I've been thinking about the future of Bloodworth Manor..."

Evelyn turned to face her son, her gaze gentle yet probing. "What's on your mind, darling?"

Edgar moved away from the window, his steps

measured as he approached her. "I want to lead differently than Father did. With compassion, with integrity. The manor shouldn't be a place of fear and secrets anymore."

A small smile tugged at Evelyn's lips. "You've grown so much, Edgar. Your father's legacy... it won't be easy to overcome."

"I know," Edgar replied, his brow furrowing. "But I've learned from you, Mother. Your strength, your kindness—that's the example I want to follow."

Evelyn reached out, clasping Edgar's hand in hers. "We'll do it together, my love. This manor has seen too much darkness. It's time to let in the light."

Their moment of connection was interrupted by a gentle knock at the door. The butler entered with a slight bow. "My lady, Miss Cecil has arrived back from her day's ride."

Evelyn's heart quickened. "Thank you, James. I'll greet her myself."

As she made her way to the entrance hall, Evelyn took a deep breath, steeling herself for the conversation ahead. Elspeth stood in the foyer, her delicate features a mixture of curiosity and apprehension.

"Elspeth, my dear," Evelyn said warmly, embracing the young woman. "I trust your time riding has gone well?"

Elspeth returned the embrace, her voice tinged with a sweetness that tugged at Evelyn's heart. "It was most wonderful, Lady Bloodworth. I was told you'd like to speak with me—is it to go over the wedding plans?"

Evelyn's smile was gentle but held a hint of something more. "We have much to discuss, but perhaps not what you're expecting. There will be no wedding. Come, let's talk somewhere more private."

As they walked towards the parlour, Evelyn's mind raced. *How does one begin to unravel a lifetime of secrets?* she wondered. The weight of the truth pressed upon her, both terrifying and liberating.

Evelyn closed the parlour door behind them, her eyes meeting Elspeth's inquisitive gaze. The room felt suddenly small, the weight of unspoken truths pressing in on them.

"Please, sit," Evelyn said, gesturing to a plush settee. She perched on the edge of an armchair opposite, her hands clasped tightly in her lap. "Elspeth, my dear, what I'm about to tell you may come as a shock, but I beg you to listen with an open heart."

Elspeth leaned forward, her brow furrowing. "Lady Bloodworth, you're worrying me. No wedding? Have I done something wrong?"

"No, dear, you have done nothing wrong." Evelyn took a deep breath, her voice trembling slightly as she began. "I'm afraid you cannot marry Edgar; you cannot marry my son. And the reason for this, you see, is that you are... you're my daughter, Elspeth. My second born child."

The words hung in the air, heavy and transformative. Elspeth's eyes widened, her lips parting in silent disbelief.

"I... I don't understand," she whispered, her hands gripping the edge of the settee.

Evelyn's eyes brimmed with tears. "It was many years ago. I was young, scared, and powerless. Julien... he could never know. It was a secret I've held for many years, and I've mourned you every day since."

As the truth sank in, Elspeth's shock gave way to a myriad of emotions. Confusion, anger, and finally, a deep, aching understanding. "All this time," she murmured, "I felt a difference in my family, but I never imagined..."

Evelyn moved to sit beside her, tentatively reaching for Elspeth's hand. "Can you ever forgive me for not finding you sooner?"

Elspeth looked at their joined hands, then into Evelyn's eyes, into her mother's eyes. In that moment, she saw not just Lady Bloodworth, but a reflection of herself—the same delicate features, the same kind heart. "There's nothing to forgive," she said softly. "You're my mother."

With those words, the dam broke. Evelyn pulled Elspeth into a fierce embrace, years of pent-up love and longing pouring out. They clung to each other, tears mingling as they began to bridge the chasm of lost time.

"Tell me everything," Elspeth said, her voice muffled against Evelyn's shoulder. "I want to know about you, about us, about all I missed."

And so, as the afternoon light softened into evening, mother and daughter shared their stories. Evelyn spoke of her own childhood, of the fear and isolation she'd endured at Bloodworth Manor, and of the strength she'd found in motherhood. Elspeth, in turn, shared tales of her life in London, the kindness of who she now knew were her adoptive family, and the yearning she'd always felt for something more.

As their conversation flowed, Elspeth's eyes shone with a new determination. "Mother," she said, the word still new and wonderful on her tongue, "I want to help you. With the manor, with everything. We've lost so much time, but now… now we can face the future together, if you'll have me?"

Evelyn cupped her daughter's face, her heart swelling with pride and love. "My darling girl," she whispered, "together, we'll bring light back to Bloodworth Manor. It's time for a new chapter—for all of us."

∞∞∞

Edgar stood before the assembled staff in the manor's great hall, his posture straight but his eyes kind. The room buzzed with a nervous energy as he cleared his throat.

"For too long, this house has been ruled by fear," he began, his voice steady. "That ends today. We aim to create an environment of mutual respect and fairness"

Maggie stepped forward. "Begging your pardon, Master Edgar, but what exactly does that mean for us?"

Edgar smiled, a warmth in his expression that reminded many of his mother. "It means fair wages, reasonable hours, and a voice in how this household is run. Your expertise is invaluable, and I want to hear your ideas."

As he spoke, Edgar couldn't help but think of his mother's strength, how she had always treated the staff with kindness despite his father's cruelty. He was determined to honour her example.

Meanwhile, in the study, Evelyn sat across from Chief Constable Thornley, who she had summoned from town as soon as possible after the girls had been freed, her gaze steady as she navigated the delicate conversation.

"These women have suffered immensely, sir," she said, her tone firm but diplomatic. "They deserve more than just freedom. They need support to rebuild their lives."

Thornley frowned. "Lady Bloodworth, while I sympathise, the logistics of such an endeavour—"

"Are complex, yes," Evelyn interjected smoothly. "But not insurmountable. I propose we establish a fund, drawn from the Bloodworth estate, to provide housing and job training... And it's Appleby Bloodworth."

As she outlined her plan, Evelyn felt a surge of confidence. She had spent years navigating Julien's moods; surely, she could handle this negotiation. The women's faces flashed in her mind, strengthening her resolve.

"Your compassion does you credit," Thornley said slowly. "But the legal implications—"

"Can be addressed," Evelyn finished. "I've taken the liberty of consulting with a solicitor. We can ensure everything is above board while still doing right by these women.

As they continued to discuss the details, Evelyn allowed herself a moment of pride. She was no longer the timid girl who had first arrived at Bloodworth Manor. She was a force to be reckoned with, fighting for those who couldn't fight for themselves, as she had always prayed someone had been able to do for her.

∞ ∞ ∞

The quill scratched softly against parchment as Evelyn penned her third letter of the evening. Candlelight flickered, casting dancing shadows across the study's mahogany desk. She paused, her eyes scanning the words she'd written to her younger sister, Beatrice.

My dearest Bea,

I know it has been far too long since last we spoke. The years have been unkind, and I bear much of the blame for our estrangement. But I write to you now with an open heart and a sincere wish to mend what has been broken.

Evelyn's hand trembled slightly as she continued writing.

I invite you, along with Mother and Father, to visit Bloodworth Manor. There is much to discuss, and even more to heal. My children, Edgar and Elspeth, long to know their family. And I... I long for the comfort of those who knew me before I became Lady Bloodworth.

Before I lost myself in it all.

She set down the quill, a familiar ache blooming in her chest. Would they even want to hear from her after all this time? The thought of rejection stung, but the possibility of reconciliation buoyed her spirit.

"I must at least try," Evelyn murmured to herself, sealing the letter with the Bloodworth crest.

As twilight deepened into night, Evelyn made her way to the manor's garden. The sweet scent of night-blooming jasmine filled the air as she approached the secluded arbour where Edgar and Elspeth waited. They sat on a wrought-iron bench, their heads bent close in quiet conversation.

"Mother," Edgar said warmly, rising to greet her. His kind eyes, so unlike his father's, searched her face. "Are you well?"

Evelyn managed a small smile. "As well as can be expected, my dear. Shall we begin?"

They settled onto the bench, Evelyn perched between her children. For a moment, only the gentle rustling of leaves and distant chirping of crickets broke the silence.

"I remember," Evelyn began hesitantly, looking toward Elspeth, "how your father and I would sneak down here on a night, and disappear into a world all of our own."

Edgar chuckled softly. "He taught me to ride, you know, on his visits. Said a gentleman should be as comfortable on a horse as in a study."

"Archie always did have a way of balancing duty with joy," Evelyn mused, her voice thick with emotion. "Do you recall how he'd sing those ridiculous sea shanties as he wandered around the manor when he thought no one was listening?"

As they shared more stories, laughter mingled with tears. Evelyn felt a warmth spreading through her chest, a bittersweet mixture of grief and gratitude. In this moment, surrounded by her children and bathed in memories of Archie's love, she allowed herself to hope for a brighter future.

Some time later, the cool night air caressed Evelyn's cheeks as she stepped onto the balcony, her eyes sweeping across the moonlit expanse of Bloodworth Manor. The estate stretched before her, a patchwork of silvery fields and shadowy woods, no longer a prison but a canvas of possibility.

She gripped the stone balustrade, her fingers tracing the weathered grooves. "So much has changed," she murmured to herself, her voice barely above a whisper.

Edgar's footsteps approached from behind. "Mother? Are you alright out here alone?"

Evelyn turned, offering her son a gentle smile. "I'm more than alright, my dear. Come, stand with me."

As Edgar joined her, she studied his profile, seeing echoes of Julien's strong features softened by a kindness his father never possessed.

"What do you see when you look out there?" she asked, gesturing to the grounds.

Edgar's brow furrowed in thought. "I see... responsibility. A legacy to uphold, but also to reshape."

Evelyn nodded, her heart swelling with pride. "Yes, exactly. But do you know what I see?"

"Tell me," Edgar urged, his voice eager.

"I see hope," Evelyn said, her tone growing stronger. "I see a future where Bloodworth Manor stands for something greater than power or tradition. A place of compassion, of healing."

She closed her eyes briefly, inhaling the crisp night air. When she opened them, there was a fierce determination in her gaze.

"We have the chance to build something beautiful here, Edgar. To right the wrongs of the past and create a legacy worthy of Archie's memory, of your empathy, of better days to come."

Edgar placed a hand on her shoulder. "We will, Mother. Together."

Evelyn covered his hand with her own, feeling a surge of love and resolve. As they stood there, bathed in moonlight, she allowed herself to truly believe in the bright future ahead—a future free from the shadows that had haunted these halls for far too long.

Chapter 17

A New Dawn

Evelyn Appleby Bloodworth stood in the centre of the grand hall surveying the flurry of activity around her. Crystal chandeliers sparkled overhead as servants bustled about arranging bouquets of lilies and hanging silk banners. A smile played at the corners of her lips as she breathed in the scent of polished wood and fresh flowers.

"My lady," a maid curtsied as she approached, "where would you like the silver trays placed?"

Evelyn's gaze softened. "Near the windows, I think. The afternoon light will make them shine beautifully."

As the maid hurried off, Evelyn's thoughts drifted. Twenty-six years ago, she had entered this very hall as a trembling bride of seventeen, overwhelmed by the opulence and grandeur of Bloodworth Manor. Now, at forty-three, she stood tall, her quiet strength filling the space that once intimidated her.

"Everything looks splendid," she murmured to herself. "Who would have thought..." She trailed off, marvelling at the transformation—not just of the hall, but of herself.

Maggie approached with a curtsy. "My lady, the kitchen staff await your approval on the menu."

"Of course," Evelyn replied, her voice warm yet authoritative. "Shall we?"

As they walked, Evelyn's hand brushed against the cool marble of a nearby column. She remembered cowering behind it once, hiding from Julien's icy stare. Now, she strode past it with confident steps.

In the bustling kitchen, Evelyn addressed the staff with a smile. "I want to express my deepest gratitude for your tireless efforts," she began, her tone both gentle and assured. "This celebration wouldn't be possible without each and every one of you."

The cook, red-faced from the heat of the ovens, beamed. "It's our pleasure, my lady. We're honoured to serve you."

Evelyn felt a swell of emotion in her chest. How far she had come from the days when the staff viewed her with pity or indifference. Now, there was genuine warmth in their eyes.

"I have every confidence that tonight will be

magnificent," she continued. "Now, let's review that menu, shall we?"

As she discussed the courses with the cook, Evelyn caught sight of her reflection in a polished copper pot. The scared girl was gone, replaced by a woman who commanded respect not through fear, but through kindness and strength. She allowed herself a moment of pride.

"My lady," Maggie interjected softly, "is everything to your liking?"

Evelyn turned, her emerald eyes bright with unshed tears of joy. "More than I could have ever imagined, Maggie. More than I could have ever dreamed."

As Evelyn finished her conversation with the housekeeper, the grand hall doors swung open, revealing Edgar's tall figuure. His kind eyes lit up as he spotted his mother, and he strode towards her with purpose.

"Mother," Edgar called, his voice filled with barely contained excitement. "I've just had the most invigorating conversation with Mr. Wood in town about our plans for the new schoolhouse."

Evelyn turned to face her son, her eyes sparkling with interest. "Do tell, my dear. What brilliant ideas have you concocted this time?"

Edgar's hands moved animatedly as he spoke. "We've devised a way to incorporate a library within the schoolhouse, open to all villagers. Imagine, Mother, the power of education freely available to everyone!"

Evelyn's heart swelled with pride. "That's wonderful, Edgar. Your father would never—" She paused, catching herself. "Well, it matters not. I believe in your vision wholeheartedly."

"There's more," Edgar continued, his voice lowering conspiratorially. "We're exploring the possibility of offering evening classes for adults who wish to further their education."

As Evelyn listened, she marvelled at her son's passion. How different he was from Julien, she thought. Where Julien saw only the preservation of power, Edgar saw the potential for positive change.

"Edgar, your dedication to using our influence for good is truly admirable," Evelyn said, reaching out to squeeze his hand. "I couldn't be more proud."

Just then, a melodious voice chimed in. "Did I hear talk of the new schoolhouse?" Elspeth approached, her eyes alight with curiosity.

"Indeed, you did," Edgar replied, turning to include her in the conversation. "We were just discussing some new initiatives."

Elspeth clasped her hands together in excitement. "Oh, how wonderful! I've been thinking about ways we could expand our charitable efforts. Perhaps, we could organise a clothing drive for the children who'll be attending?"

Evelyn watched as Edgar and Elspeth began to exchange ideas, their enthusiasm infectious. She felt a warmth spread through her chest, realising how seamlessly Elspeth had become a part of their family since she'd suggested her newfound daughter move in with them permanently. They had plenty of room now she'd instructed the staff to open and clear out the many bedrooms the manor had to offer.

"That's an excellent idea, Elspeth," Evelyn interjected. "Your compassion never ceases to amaze me."

Elspeth blushed at the compliment. "I only wish to contribute in any way I can. This estate has given me so much; it's only right that we extend that generosity to others."

As the conversation flowed, Evelyn found herself marvelling at the scene before her. Here, in the very hall where she had once felt so alone, stood her son and daughter, two bright lights of hope for the future. They represented everything she had ever dreamed of for Bloodworth Manor— compassion, progress, and above all, love. And to think, once upon a time, she had thought running away was the only escape possible.

∞∞∞

Evelyn's eyes scanned the parchment before her, the flickering candlelight casting a warm glow across the library's mahogany desk. She dipped her quill into the inkwell, making precise notations in the ledger. The familiar scent of leather-bound books and aged paper enveloped her, a comforting embrace as she worked.

"If we reallocate funds from the eastern fields," she murmured to herself, "we could expand the apprenticeship program without compromising the harvest." Her brow furrowed in concentration, mind racing with possibilities.

A gentle knock at the door interrupted her thoughts. "Come in," Evelyn called, her voice carrying a hint of curiosity.

The door creaked open, revealing a tall, distinguished gentleman with salt-and-pepper hair and kind eyes. "Lady Bloodworth," he said, bowing slightly. "I hope I'm not intruding."

Evelyn's heart skipped a beat as she recognised Lord Jonathan Fairfax, the widower from the neighbouring estate, who she had met a handful of times during the grand parties and feasts she'd had to organise over the years. "Not at all, Lord Fairfax. And it's Lady Appleby Bloodworth now." She replied, rising from her seat. "Please, do come in."

As he approached, Evelyn noticed a small, wrapped package in his hands. "I wanted to offer my condolences for your loss," he said softly, "and to wish you a happy birthday. Though, I do suppose doing both at once may have been indelicate of me."

Evelyn felt a flush creep up her neck. "That's very kind of you, Jonathan," she said, surprised by the ease with which his first name slipped from her lips, suddenly wondering if she should have used his title, as he had hers.

He extended the gift, their fingers brushing as she accepted it. "It's nothing grand, I'm afraid," he said with a self-deprecating smile. "Just a book I thought you might enjoy."

As Evelyn unwrapped the package, revealing a beautifully bound copy of sonnets, she found herself thinking: *How thoughtful. He remembers my love of poetry, even from our limited conversations over the years.*

Aloud, she said, "Thank you, it's lovely."

Their eyes met and, for a moment, Evelyn felt a flutter in her chest she hadn't experienced in years—not since she'd first set eyes on Archie. *Perhaps,* she thought, *there's still room for new chapters in my own story.*

∞∞∞

The manor's grand dining room buzzed with life, a stark contrast to the sombre atmosphere that had lingered for so long. Evelyn stood at the threshold, her emerald eyes wide with wonder as she took in the scene before her. Laughter echoed off the high ceilings, mingling with the soft strains of a string quartet.

"My lady," the butler approached, offering a flute of champagne. "The guests are all eager to wish you a happy birthday."

Evelyn accepted the glass, her fingers trembling slightly.

"Thank you, James," she murmured, taking a sip to steady her nerves. As she glanced around the room, she caught sight of Lord Fairfax engaged in animated conversation with some of the local gentry.

"I never thought I'd see Bloodworth Manor like this," she mused, a small smile playing on her lips. The room was awash with colour, from the vibrant floral arrangements to the elegant gowns of the ladies in attendance. It was as if life itself had returned to the estate. And that colours other than red existed once again.

As Evelyn made her way through the crowd,

accepting birthday wishes and engaging in pleasant conversation, she couldn't help but feel a sense of pride. This was her doing—the transformation of Bloodworth Manor from a place of darkness to one of light and hope.

Suddenly, the music changed, and Lord Fairfax appeared at her side. "Lady Appleby Bloodworth," he said, his warm eyes twinkling, "might I have the honour of this dance?"

Evelyn hesitated for a moment, her heart racing. *It's been so long,* she thought. *Can I truly allow myself this happiness after everything? After Archie?*

Aloud, she replied, "I would be delighted, Lord Fairfax."

As he led her to the dance floor, Evelyn felt the eyes of the room upon them. His hand rested lightly on her waist, and as they began to move in time with the music, she found herself relaxing into his embrace.

"You've done wonders with the estate," Lord Fairfax murmured, his voice low and intimate. "It's as if the very walls are breathing again."

Evelyn's cheeks flushed at the compliment, realising for the first time that even outsiders had noticed to some extent the suffocating presence that she'd lived in for so long. "Thank you," she replied. "It hasn't been easy, but it's been worth every moment."

As they twirled across the floor, Evelyn allowed herself to truly look at Lord Fairfax. The kindness in his eyes, the gentle strength of his hand holding hers—it all spoke of a man far different from the one she had known before... and yet reminded her so much of another she had held so tightly.

Perhaps, she thought, her heart fluttering, *there's room in my life for more than just duty and responsibility. Maybe, just maybe, there's room for love, too.*

The dance ended all too soon, and as Lord Fairfax bowed, Evelyn found herself wishing for just one more turn around the floor. As they parted, she caught a glimpse of her reflection in a nearby mirror—cheeks flushed, eyes bright, looking more alive than she had in years.

"Happy birthday, indeed," she whispered to herself, a cautious smile spreading across her face as she turned back to her guests, ready to embrace whatever the future might hold.

The cool evening air caressed Evelyn's skin as she stepped into the gardens, the lively chatter of the celebration fading behind her. Edgar and Elspeth flanked her sides, their footsteps crunching softly on the gravel path. Moonlight bathed the manicured hedges and blooming roses in an ethereal glow, casting long shadows across the lawn.

"It's hard to believe how much has changed," Evelyn mused, scanning over the tranquil landscape. "This garden was once a symbol of escape from oppression, holding nothing more than where I could go when I could not bear to be anywhere else, but now..."

Edgar nodded, his expression thoughtful. "Now it's a place of hope, Mother. A testament to what we can achieve together."

Elspeth's gentle voice chimed in, "I never imagined a place could transform so completely, even from my limited time here at the manor. It's inspiring."

As they meandered along the path, Evelyn felt a swell of pride. "What are your thoughts on our next steps, Edgar? You mentioned some ideas earlier."

Edgar's eyes lit up, his posture straightening with enthusiasm. "I've been in talks with several local leaders," he began, his words measured but brimming with excitement. "There's a growing interest in establishing the school I mentioned earlier, for the children of tenant farmers. I believe we could use part of the estate to house it."

Evelyn raised an eyebrow, intrigued. "That's quite ambitious. How do you envision it working?"

"We'd start small," Edgar explained, gesturing animatedly. "Perhaps, with basic reading and arithmetic. But in time, we could expand to include more advanced subjects, even vocational training."

As Edgar spoke, Evelyn couldn't help but marvel at the man he'd become. Gone was the uncertain boy, replaced by a passionate advocate for change. She felt a lump form in her throat, overcome with a mixture of pride and bittersweet nostalgia.

"It's a wonderful idea," Evelyn said softly, reaching out to squeeze her son's hand. "I'm so proud of the man you've become, Edgar."

A shadow of emotion flickered across Edgar's face before he smiled. "Thank you, Mother. I hope to use our family's influence for good, to make a real difference in people's lives."

As they continued their stroll, Evelyn's mind raced with possibilities. The Bloodworth name, once associated with cruelty and oppression, could become a beacon of progress and hope. It was a legacy she could embrace wholeheartedly.

"We'll need to tread carefully," Evelyn cautioned, her years of experience tempering her excitement. "Change often breeds resistance, especially among those accustomed to the old ways."

Edgar nodded solemnly. "I understand. But I'm prepared for the challenge. With your guidance and support, I believe we can overcome any obstacle."

As they rounded a corner, the manor came back into view, its windows aglow with warmth and celebration. Evelyn paused, taking in the sight of her home—no longer a prison, but a symbol of transformation and new beginnings.

"Together," she said, her voice filled with quiet determination, "we'll build a future worthy of the new Bloodworth name."

Elspeth, who had been listening intently, her delicate features illuminated by the soft glow of the garden lanterns, stepped forward. Her eyes sparkled with enthusiasm as she addressed Evelyn and Edgar.

"I'd love to learn more about the estate's charitable efforts," she said, her voice gentle yet earnest. "Perhaps, I could assist in some way? I've always felt drawn to helping those in need."

Evelyn smiled warmly at the young woman, touched by her compassion. "Of course, my dear. We'd be delighted to have your help. There's so much to be done."

Edgar nodded in agreement. "Elspeth, your kindness would be invaluable. We'd love your help with the school for underprivileged children in the village. Your experience in London could bring a fresh perspective."

Elspeth's face lit up with excitement. "The

school? That's wonderful! I could teach reading and writing or, perhaps, help with organising supplies."

As Elspeth and Edgar eagerly discussed potential projects, Evelyn found herself hanging back slightly, watching her children with a profound sense of pride. The cool evening air caressed her face as she observed their animated conversation, their laughter drifting on the breeze.

They've grown so much, Evelyn thought, her heart swelling with emotion. *Not only in years, but in spirit and character.*

She recalled the frightened, uncertain child her son had once been, trapped in the suffocating atmosphere of Julien's reign; the daughter she had given up as an infant. Now, here they stood —Edgar, a man of conviction and purpose, and Elspeth, now back in her life, brimming with compassion and eagerness to make a difference.

Evelyn's eyes misted as she listened to their plans, their voices filled with hope and determination. She had nurtured her son through dark times, protected them both fiercely in the only ways she knew how, and now she was witnessing the fruits of her love and sacrifice.

"Mother?" Edgar's voice broke through her reverie. "Are you alright?"

Evelyn blinked away her tears, offering a radiant smile. "More than alright, my darlings.

I'm simply... overwhelmed with joy, seeing the remarkable people you've become."

Momentarily, Evelyn looked away from her children, drawn to the edge of the gardens where the manicured lawns gave way to rolling hills. The setting sun cast a golden glow over Bloodworth Manor, its once-forbidding silhouette now a beacon of warmth and possibility. She inhaled deeply, the scent of roses mingling with the earthy aroma of freshly tilled soil from the newly established community gardens.

"It's breathtaking, isn't it?" Edgar's voice came from behind her. "I can hardly believe it's the same place."

Evelyn turned back, her eyes shining in the moonlight. "It's not just the estate that's transformed, my dear. We all have."

Elspeth joined them, linking her arm through Evelyn's. "You made this possible, Mother. Your strength... it's inspired all of us."

A lump formed in Evelyn's throat. She gazed out over the land again, memories of darker days flashing through her mind—the isolation, the fear, the seemingly insurmountable challenges. Yet here she stood, not just surviving, but thriving.

"There were times I thought I'd break," Evelyn admitted softly. "But every trial, every hardship... they've forged something in me I never knew existed."

Edgar placed a gentle hand on her shoulder. "You've shown us what true resilience looks like."

Evelyn smiled, her voice gaining strength. "And now, we have the freedom to shape our future. To love, to grow, to make a difference in ways we've only just begun to imagine."

As twilight deepened, casting long shadows across the grounds, Evelyn felt a profound sense of peace settle over her. The journey had been long and fraught with peril, but standing here, with her family by her side and endless possibilities stretching before them, she knew that every step had been worth it.

"Come," she said, turning to embrace her children. "Let's go inside. Tomorrow is a new day, and I can't wait to see what it brings."

As they walked back towards the warmly lit manor, Evelyn's heart swelled with hope and anticipation. The story of Bloodworth Manor—their story—was far from over. It was, she realised with quiet joy, only truly just beginning.

About The Author

Iona Stuart

Iona Stuart is a freelance proofreader and marketing executive. She is known for her love of exploring life through poetry, language, and literature; ever on the quest to find the 'right' words to express the meaning of life, the world, and everything.

Printed in Great Britain
by Amazon